Return to Skunk Corners

Rebecca M. Douglass

This is a work of fiction. Names, characters, places, and incidents are products of the author's imagination and are not to be construed as real. Any resemblance to actual events, locales, organizations, or persons, living or dead, is entirely coincidental.

Copyright © 2013 Rebecca M. Douglass
Cover illustration by Danielle English
http://www.kanizo.co.uk
Cover design by Steven Tse
Interior illustrations © Walter Merchant

ISBN: 1490560742
ISBN-13: 978-1490560748

DEDICATION

To Dad.

I miss you every day.

CONTENTS

ACKNOWLEDGMENTS

Books don't happen in a vacuum, and this one is no exception. I want to thank Library Laurie for once again encouraging (demanding) me to write more stories (and proof-reading the final document, an exacting job for which I am immensely grateful), and all the old library staff for their support of my writing. Huge thanks to Lisa Frieden for editorial services, and to Danielle English for the cover art, Steven Tse for cover design, and Walter Merchant for the skunks leading off each chapter. I also want to thank my readers who keep telling me they like it—nothing makes a writer want to write like knowing someone wants to read it. Finally, thanks to my husband and sons who put up with me spending ever more time writing, and less doing those Mom things they thought they could expect.

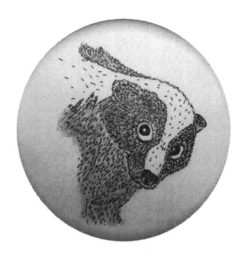

1 SKUNK CORNERS WITH NO LIBRARIAN

It didn't come as any surprise. When we sent the toughs from Endoline packing without any help from the Skunk Corners librarian, I knew what we'd proven. I'd known the Ninja Librarian long enough to guess what came next.

Still, it had been a nasty shock when I woke that morning to find an envelope on my kitchen table. Only one person could've snuck in and left it without me waking. With a sinking feeling, I slit the envelope with my hunting knife, feeling the big brass key inside. Along with the key to the library was a single line penned on a bit of stationery in the Ninja Librarian's fussy, old-fashioned handwriting:

It's yours now, Alice.

Mine? I knew even less about running a library than I did about running a school. Which, despite several years in charge of the Skunk Corners school, wasn't much. Anyway, I couldn't run a library *and* a school, could I? I raced to the library, meaning to stop him if I had to sit on him, but he was gone.

Just like that, I'd lost my best friend, my teacher, and my mentor, and gained another unwanted responsibility. If Ninja Tom wanted me to grow up, he'd opted for the sink-or-swim approach.

I was giving some serious thought to sinking.

It wasn't just me. In the following weeks my students grew mopey, the mayor nervous, and Tess and her girls cranky. Maybe not as cranky as me, but they'd lost a friend, too. Like me, they didn't have many they could spare.

In short, our town had lost its heart, just when we'd started to learn we had one.

"This is silly," Tess tried to convince us both. We were having drinks in her place—Two-Timin' Tess's Tavern—shortly before closing a couple weeks after he left. We sipped our tea from shot glasses. "It's not like Tom was one of us," she argued. "We got on before he came. We'll get on without him."

"I know," I said. "He was just an outsider who came and tried to tell us how to run things." It was a good effort, but it didn't work. "I was an outsider myself not so long ago. Tess. What makes me any different from him?" Tess shrugged. She didn't have any answers.

Ninja Tom had come and shown our whole town how to grow up, and that was worth a whole lot more than being born here. Everything was different because of him, and what I was afraid of—what we all feared—was that without him we couldn't keep it up.

"I don't want Skunk Corners to go back to being the sort of town that drives off librarians and raises children who can't read. *Won't* read, which you've gotta admit is worse."

"I know," Tess said.

"That's why I've been so gloomy and

cantankerous."

I suppose I should introduce myself. Around Skunk Corners I'm known as Big Al, though Tom called me by my given name almost from the first. That's one thing Tom hadn't finished before he left. I might've let him call me Alice—he once kicked me into the street on my hindquarters for backtalk, so I didn't argue—but he couldn't make me like the name. And I didn't let anyone else use it. Now that he was gone, no one called me Alice, not even Tess, who dared most things.

Tom hadn't managed to turn Big Al into a girl. It should have made me happy.

Later that night, though my heart wasn't in it, I practiced the drills Tom had taught me. That was another thing he hadn't finished. I was no Ninja fighter yet, though I was better set to defend myself than I'd been a year before. I could maybe handle the sort of trouble-maker we got here well enough. I'd already kicked one low-down side-winder out of town. But I'd be no match for someone really mean.

And I didn't know how to defend Skunk Corners from itself. Fewer people came to the library now, and I didn't seem to have Tom's ability to captivate the children at story time. Oh, I knew the tricks he'd used in the beginning. But he hadn't needed those tricks for long. His voice could hold them once they'd been quiet long enough to hear it. Mine held no magic at all.

So I was expecting the worst when disaster hit our town, though what I expected was nothing like what happened.

That afternoon, the hail hit right along with the first of the thunder, a crack loud enough and close enough to shake the school, if the wind hadn't already been shaking it. Within moments every window on the west side of the schoolhouse was broken, and hail mixed with the broken glass on the floor. Half the kids were screaming or crying, or both, but I rounded everyone up and we huddled in the corner of the room farthest from the broken windows while the rain and hail pounded in and the wind shook the building.

"Don't you worry," I soothed the kids. "This school is built pretty tough."

Listening to the wind, I thought I might have been lying. At least we didn't have trees hanging over us. Other buildings in town wouldn't be so lucky. "Soon's this dies down, everyone in town will be out checking on folks and helping each other, and we can see what we can do, too."

For one brief moment I allowed myself a doubt. That wasn't really the Skunk Corners way. There'd been little enough of working together and helping out in this town over the years.

Until the Ninja Librarian had come.

Tom had taught us to act like a town, and we'd proven we could, clearing out a batch of toughs from up the mountain who thought they could take over. We'd done it with brains and humor and teamwork, and we'd been proud of ourselves.

Then Tom left.

Were we still a town, or were we just a bunch of cantankerous misfits?

When the wind and rain began to die away, we got up from our huddle, ready to shy if a new threat emerged. My oldest students scrounged for things to stick over the broken windows to keep out the wind and rain. Another found and lit the lamp. The clouds made it that dark, though it was only midafternoon and well into May.

I looked over the mess, then got to work. Janey Holstead and MaryBeth Burton, the Fifth Reader class, gathered the little kids on the far side of the room, away from the broken windows. Sarah,

Eunice, and Joey, all old enough to be careful, I set to sweeping the mess of hail and glass into a pile. I scooped the wet shards into buckets myself. As soon as the room was safe for the little ones, I told the girls they were in charge. They all wanted to come out, but it wasn't time yet, with rain still falling and who-knew-what waiting out there.

Instead, I just took the Sixth Reader class—hulking, nearly-adult Hank and Yance, and twelve-year-old thinkers Tommy and Peggy—out to study the damage. We stopped in the entry and looked out at the rain, which was slacking some but still wet. No one had brought a slicker to school, it being nigh on to summer. I shrugged and led the way out into the muddy street.

Skunk Corners was a shambles. The library, our town's one brick building, stood solid. But every other building in town had suffered. We saw broken windows all over, and fallen trees crushing roofs and porches. We stood there a minute, just staring. Other folks began to come out of their houses and whatnot. Like us, they looked this way and that, as though we didn't quite know this strange, changed world.

The rain tapered off, the storm breaking up or moving on, the way spring weather does. I finished my examination of the street and gasped.

A tree had fallen onto Two-Timin' Tess's Tavern, crushing half the barroom, and completely blocking the door, if the door was even still there. It seemed to have missed the upstairs, which was set back from the front of the building, but the bar was where people would be. I gave a holler to get everyone's attention and gestured at the Tavern even as the kids and I broke into a run.

"Tess! Johnny! Anyone alive in there?" Tommy was already on the porch and yelling for all he was worth. I kept going around to the back, hoping to find someone in the kitchen.

I couldn't tell, because another tree had fallen there, blocking the door with a two-foot trunk and a mess of branches so thick I couldn't get anywhere near. Rounding the front corner again, I hollered, "Some of you folk get saws! I'm gonna try the window." No answering yells met me, and Peggy grabbed my arm.

"What?" I snapped.

Mutely, she waved a hand down the street. No one had come a-runnin' when I yelled. No one was coming at all. Folks worked away at their own messes, each struggling alone.

A wave of anger swept over me. What were they doing? We were a town, dag nab it! We worked together on what needed doing.

Didn't we?

This was no time to think about that. Hank ran off for the saw and axe at the school, and Tommy went to wriggle through the mess out back to get at Tess's woodshed and find hers. Peg, Yance, and I circled to the window on the undamaged side of the Tavern and tried to peer in. The ground sloped away some on that side, and the window was too high even for me, so we boosted Peggy until she could see.

"Johnny!" she called, and to my relief Tess's bartender appeared a moment later. His face was pale where it wasn't bloody, but he was alive and moving.

"Gawd, Johnny, are you alive?" That was Yance. There's a reason he's still in school at his age.

I asked a better question. "Where're the girls? Are they okay?"

Johnny touched his head like it hurt, which I'm sure it did, given the amount of blood. "I—I'm not sure. I think they're in the kitchen. I can't get to the door. Check around back."

"It's no good. You can't get to the kitchen from in there?"

"Nope." He carefully didn't shake his head to indicate the negative.

"Holler and see if they answer."

Johnny moved out of sight, and I could hear him call, "Tess? Tildy? Anyone?" More faintly, I could hear a muffled voice responding. "You all okay?" Johnny called again.

In a minute he reappeared at the window. "They're fine, but stuck. Both doors blocked." And there were no windows in the kitchen, except one alongside the blocked door. That one likely had a branch sticking right through, way things were going.

Hank and Tommy had come back. Hank had a saw and two axes, but Tommy was empty-handed.

"I couldn't get through, Teacher!"

I sent him and Peggy for a ladder from wherever they could scrounge one, and had Hank and Yance— at seventeen they were plenty big—boost me to the window.

I surveyed the mess inside. It was bad, but I thought we'd be better off here than around back. It'd take us days to cut through the massive oak trunk that lay against the back door. Inside, there was a mess of branches from the oak that used to shade the south side of the Tavern. The trunk had flattened the outer part of the barroom.

The boys gave me a shove, and I hauled myself over the sill and landed in a heap at Johnny's feet. Scrambling up, I turned and leaned out for the tools. Looking down the street I saw Tommy and Peggy coming with a ladder they'd scrounged somewhere, so I didn't have to hoist the boys through the window. Thank heavens for that.

I took a closer look at Johnny as he reached for an axe, and pulled it away from him. "You don't look so good. That thing knock you out?"

He nodded, and his grimace said that hadn't been a good idea. I handed him my handkerchief, wet through from the still-heavy rain, like everything I wore. He wiped the blood from his face, then knotted the cloth over the cut on his forehead.

"Better stick with the saw. You might not be seeing straight." I didn't try to tell him to sit down and take care of himself. Tess and the girls were family, in whatever ways mattered, and no one else was coming to help. We needed his strong arms. I just didn't want him to cut off a foot along the way.

We set to work like beavers, Tess calling encouragement from the other side of the kitchen door. In a few minutes, during which we'd cut a small pile of branches—with Tommy and Peg to drag them out of the way so we could keep axes and saws going—the kitchen door kind of fell open. Tess and Tildy had removed the doorjamb and pulled the whole door loose. Now they could pull away more debris, using a couple of big kitchen knives to hack off the small branches. Annie keeps her knives sharp. In short order we'd made enough of a path to get them all out over the mess: Tess and Tildy, Julia and Hilda, and Annie, the cook.

Belatedly, I thought to ask if there'd been any customers in the Tavern. If there had been, they'd've been right about where the tree was now. To my relief, Tess shook her head.

"We hadn't opened, on account of the storm."

We all went back to studying the mess. Hilda started for the door, but Johnny just pointed at the window. The front door was still blocked. Well, not so much blocked as crushed. Gone.

Tess was quiet for a long time, and I wondered what she was thinking as she looked from the wreck of her tavern to the motley crew of children who'd rescued them. We watched to see what she would do. Another woman might've sat down and had herself a cry, but that's not Tess's way. I thought maybe she'd get right to work cleaning up her Tavern.

"Well," Tess said at last. "Let's get out there and see who needs help."

Tommy said what I was thinking. "Why, Miss Tess? They ain't in any hurry to help you, not so's I can see."

Tess looked from him to me and my other pupils. We all nodded. She set her jaw. "That's no excuse. Some out there'll need help, and we're going to give it." Echoing my earlier thoughts, but without a trace of the bitterness or doubt I felt, she added, "We're a town and we work together at what needs doing."

Would believing that make it true again?

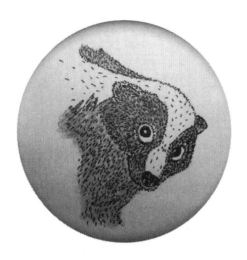

2 SKUNK CORNERS CLEANS UP

The rain had stopped, and we'd rescued Tess's crew from what was left of Two-Timin' Tess's Tavern. But Skunk Corners was still a mess. The lot of us, my students who'd rescued Tess, and her whole crew, stood in the street, looking back and forth from the ruined watering hole to our shambles of a town.

Tess moved first. Mrs. Herberts had come out of the Tea Shop, which was a fancy name for the front room of her house, where a body could buy a sandwich and a bowl of soup. The wind had torn the roof half off the little building, and though the rain had stopped, something had to be done, and soon, or Mrs. Herberts would lose everything. Maybe Tess figured that, as a widow with no man around, she needed help the most. Maybe it was just the first thing she saw that needed doing. At any rate, Tess led us all down the street to her shop.

Certainly, Mrs. Herberts looked like she could use our help. She sort of slumped as she studied the damage.

"It's a terrible mess. I don't know what I'll do." Then she looked down the street and straightened her back. "Big Al, you run on down to the Holstead's and make sure Jane and little James Thomas are safe."

The firm command didn't surprise me, despite how hopeless she'd looked a moment before. James Thomas belonged to all of us, but to Mrs. Herberts next after the Holsteads. He'd been left on the library steps a few months back, and Jane Holstead and her husband Ike had adopted him, but Mrs. Herberts had wanted him something fierce.

I found Mrs. Holstead sweeping up glass and mopping water from her floor. I looked at James Thomas, happily playing with his toes in his cradle, and asked if she needed any help.

"I thank you for coming, Big Al. No, we're just fine. Mr. Holstead isn't home, but he'll be back by night, and we only suffered a bit of broken glass. You go and help someone who needs it."

As I turned to go, she added, "Are all the children safe?"

"Yes ma'am. We cleaned up the glass, and your Janey is helping keep the little 'uns in. We won't let them go home til it's safe, so I need Janey a bit longer, if you don't mind." Glancing down the street, I could see that some parents were heading for the school—town folk like Mrs. Mayor Burton and Eunice's ma.

I made my way back to Mrs. Herberts' place, stopping on the way to help Mr. Johnson cut loose the big "Johnson's Mercantile" sign which now dangled over his door like the Sword of Damocles. That's in the Sixth Reader. Anyway, we didn't want the sign to fall on anyone.

By the time I reached the rest of my crew, Mrs. Burton was there just a-waiting for me. Her daughter was not with her.

"What is the meaning of this, Big Al?" she asked indignantly.

"Well, there seems to have been a big storm," I began. She was not amused, and looked down her nose at me. Since I am taller than she is, she had to tilt her head back to do it. I thought that rather ruined the effect.

"I went to collect my daughter, to be sure she is well, and she tells me she cannot leave. That you put her and little Janey Holstead in charge and they have to keep the other children safe."

"That's right."

"Go tell my child she is to come with me!"

I shook my head. "MaryBeth is doing her part. Someone has to watch the little 'uns until they can go home."

"That is your job," Mrs. Burton huffed.

"I'm needed out here, and my older students too." I gestured at the ruin the storm had made of our town. "People may be hurt." Realizing that might be true, I turned back to my students. "Let's spread out and check all the buildings. Find out if anyone's trapped or hurt."

A noise caused me to turn back to Mrs. Burton, who huffed, "That is not your job!"

"No, I suppose it isn't." Tess spoke from behind me. "I suppose it's your husband's job. He is the mayor. But as Al is a citizen of this town and sees a need, I guess she's right to fill it."

Mrs. Burton huffed again, but, finding no sympathizers, turned and marched back down the street, disappearing through her fancy front door and slamming it behind her.

Five minutes later, I emerged from the church, where I'd found Preacher Dawson flustered but unhurt. Mayor Burton strode up the street past me, gathering the men with calls and waves of his hand. Now that the worst was past—and it was an important man asking—they came.

"Gentlemen," he pronounced, "we need to organize a search to be certain all—" we didn't hear what he might have said, because Tommy ran up yelling.

"Teacher, ain't nobody hurt that we can find, but ol' Miss Cornelia's roof 'most come off, and I think someone's stuck in the privy behind the bank. It blew over and there's a sight of yellin' and cussin' out there."

"Well?" I turned to the mayor and waited.

As when we'd cleared the toughs from town, Mayor Burton was not unwilling to act when the right path was pointed out to him. He and a half-dozen men took off to help Miss Cornelia. Being old and all, she'd never be able to fix her roof alone, any more than Mrs. Herberts would. Hank and Yance were already starting to clear the ruined parts of that, so someone could make repairs.

Before leaving, the mayor ordered, "Al, you take some of your young folk and go right that privy."

It figured. He wouldn't want to tackle a job like that. I would have protested, but Tommy winked at me, so I waited to see what was up.

"It's Mr. Tolliver in there," he announced as soon as the mayor was gone, and we took off wearing matching grins. Hank, Yance, and a couple of the younger men decided to follow us and see the fun. I probably should have sent Peggy off so she wouldn't hear unfitting language, but I didn't.

The banker was no one's favorite, being a tight-fisted stuffed shirt with no sense of humor. Seemed to me he'd been known to chide folks for bad language, too. No wonder the boys wanted witnesses to his foul—and foul-mouthed—

predicament.

Somehow, in the process of freeing the banker, and purely by accident, the outhouse rolled over a couple of extra times. When Tolliver finally emerged, his frock coat was dirty and his pants torn, though at least he had managed to pull them up. Since he emerged spewing threats and blaming us for taking so long, we figured he was well enough. We left to go help someone more deserving.

For one fleeting moment I wondered if the Ninja Librarian would have approved of what we'd just done, but squelched the doubt. We were here, and he wasn't. Besides, I thought he might've enjoyed it, even if he didn't approve.

By dark, we'd checked up on everyone in town and most of the outlying homes. We'd done enough to the roofs to keep the weather out, mostly, and all of my little students had been retrieved—except Billy Jenkins. Hank and Yance had left under protest, reclaimed by their ma, who said she needed their help on their own place. Tommy and Peggy didn't go, nor did anyone come asking for them.

Tommy pulled me aside. "I think its best if Billy don't go home noways," he whispered. "Since Jake ain't been around, his ma's been powerful cranky." By which I figured he meant she was usually drunk by nightfall. Mr. Jenkins had decamped the previous fall for parts unknown. Crazy Jake Jenkins had been looking after his nephew some, but he and Wild Harry Colson had recently gone to take work on the railroad. That was a triumph and a marvel, but seemed like everything came with a price.

I looked around the school, thinking aloud. "It's a long way to your place, or his. Or yours," I added, looking at Peggy. Her parents let her run wild, and likely wouldn't worry that she hadn't come home. I thought some more, ideas coming slowly, tired as I was. The school was a mess, and Tess's place wouldn't be habitable for some time. We'd all need a warm, dry place to stay.

"We'll all bunk at the library," I decided. "Fetch the bedding from my room, and we'll be here all ready to get the school cleaned up tomorrow." I left the kids to get the blankets, and went to tell Tess.

She showed, for the first time since I'd known her, signs of fatigue and discouragement, but brightened considerably when I put my plan to her.

"Why, thank you, Al. Annie's gone to help Mrs. Herberts—I do hope I'll get her back; those two could talk food all night!—and Tildy's helping Mrs. Holstead. Her man's not made it back and we didn't like to leave her alone with just Janey and the baby. But the rest of us accept with pleasure. A bite to eat and a dry corner would be heaven just now." She looked from her muddy, bedraggled skirts to those of Hilda and Julia, and sighed. "Well, clean clothes would be nice, but there's no getting at our rooms just yet."

I answered without thinking. "I've some extra." Then I added, seeing the women glance at one another and afraid I might have offended them, "If you don't mind dungarees and overalls, I guess."

Julia giggled, and quickly put a hand over her mouth. "I'm sorry, Al. I'd be happy just to wear anything dry right now, but," she gestured helplessly, and I looked down at her, puzzled. When Peg looked from Julia to me and started to giggle, I saw her point, and burst out in my first good laugh in weeks. They don't call me Big Al because I'm scrawny and undersized.

"Well, you and Peggy could share," I suggested to the young woman, who was scarcely larger than the girl. "There'd be room enough for two, and you'd be warmer."

We must've all needed a laugh, because we

dissolved into helpless hoots, even though it wasn't really that funny.

But once I'd let everyone into the library, a little chilly but dry, I went back to my room and stacked every stitch I owned into my washtub. The kids had already taken the blankets, of which I had none too many. With a sigh for the boiler that had blown up last winter without producing a single hot bath, I crossed back to the library, feeling pretty low. The place was a mess and everything was all wrong.

I felt better as soon as I got inside the library. A fire in the stove drove the chill out, lamps had been lit, and Tess stirred a large pot of soup she said Mrs. Herberts had sent along. Billy was already nodding in a corner, and Peg and Tommy fought to stay awake long enough to clean up and eat. I passed out blankets and clothes, and Johnny and Tommy disappeared with the washtubs and a kettle of hot water. We left Billy to sleep. He'd not been out in the mud.

When the fellows were finished with the tubs, Hilda and Julia took Peggy to see what could be done about the mud. Hilda and Johnny were able to wear my clothes, and Tommy pretended he could, but Julia and Peggy had to improvise with blankets. Just as well. I had none too many blankets, but I hadn't too many pairs of pants, either. I hoped there was a pair left for me.

Tess and I retreated to the tubs only when we'd eaten everything there was, and the others chased us off so they could do the dishes. I gave a great sigh of contentment as I sank into my tub, however skimpy. Tess echoed me from the other washtub, and we scrubbed in silence for a few minutes. Finally, I asked,

"Tess? What will you do now?" I held my breath and waited for the answer. It was a long time coming. Finally, she sighed.

"Rebuild."

"Why?" It was the answer I wanted, but I wasn't sure why she'd given it. She didn't have a Tavern anymore, and what was there to hold her to our town? Plenty of folks said nasty things about her, and look how they'd left her to shift for herself today.

And I knew that if she left so soon after the Ninja Librarian, Skunk Corners and I were both doomed.

"Al, honey, me and the girls, we've no place else to go. The Tavern doesn't make much to support six of us, but we get by. You know what we'd be stuck with if we went anywhere else."

I did. They'd be stuck with what I'd long believed they did at the Tavern. It had turned out I was wrong, and I still wondered why Tess needed so many helpers if not for that. Not to mention how she supported them all.

"Do you suppose anyone will help you rebuild? After all you and the girls and Johnny did for them today?"

"Maybe. Maybe not. It doesn't really matter. This town is struggling, but folk are mostly decent, deep down." She paused, and while I wondered how deep you had to go to find the decent in people like Mrs. Burton, Tess started to chuckle. While I stared, bewildered, she quoted the Ninja Librarian's favorite line:

"Does that completely answer your question?"

Torn between laughter and tears, I nodded. "For the moment."

3 TRAINS RETURN TO SKUNK CORNERS

When the great storm was two days gone and still no train steamed up the tracks, folks in Skunk Corners began to fret. It wasn't just that we needed things—like window glass—but because of folks like Mr. Holstead, who was to have come in on the train the very day of the storm.

I worried a bit, too, about Crazy Jake Jenkins and Wild Harry Colson, but aside from maybe Harry's little brother Tommy, I was probably the only one. Those boys were on a lot of folk's bad side after the incident with the Drunk Swede Mine, not to mention the rest of their long history of trouble. Still, they were doing their best, and since I'd been teaching them, I counted them among my responsibilities. They were a few years older than me, but I swear those boys needed a keeper.

At first, we were all so busy cutting up the fallen trees and cleaning up the debris that we didn't have time to think much about the missing. It took a gang of us two days to put a new roof on the tea shop, while Mr. Mayor Burton told another bunch how to mend Miss Cornelia's cabin. The mayor didn't do a lot of work himself, but I must admit he organized it well.

So it was a couple of days before some of us realized there was something to worry about. School wasn't keeping. I'd canceled it until we got things cleaned up and the town back on its feet, and I was hoping for some window glass, soon's the train came in. On account of not having school, I didn't see Janey Holstead or her ma.

When I stopped for a breather on the second afternoon, I looked up the street just in time to see Janey come out of her house. She must have been on some errand, but she paused a long moment and stared down the train tracks. From my perch on Mrs. Herberts' roof I could see a fair way down the canyon, and there was nothing there. It took me a moment to realize that was the problem: nothing there. No train. No Mr. Holstead.

My first thought was to climb down and go to her right away. I'm the teacher. I'm supposed to protect my pupils, as well as teach them. What stopped me was the realization that I had no idea how to protect Janey from this.

I can knock a bad guy flying, and I'll wrassle a mountain lion if need be. I can even figure my way to getting my students fed and clothed. At least— and my thoughts faltered a bit here—I had done all that with the help of the Ninja Librarian.

But I had no idea how to heal a dreadful fear or comfort frightened people.

Of course, what I wanted to do was reach down the mountain and drag the train right up to town, and Mr. Holstead with it. But I couldn't.

When I finally came down off that roof, I wanted to just run away. *The way Tom had done*, some part of my mind said. How he'd left us to manage on our own, even though we had so little idea how. No, I wasn't that kind of coward.

At least I went to see Janey and her ma. I figure that was something.

Of course, when I got there I had no idea what to say. So I didn't say much of anything. Between them, they had managed to tack some oilcloth crookedly over the windows, and I fixed that up a little. Then I chopped a mess of firewood. Janey could split kindling just fine, but the big pieces were a lot for her to handle. When I finished that, I hugged Janey and little James Thomas, and patted Mrs. Holstead on the shoulder, not knowing if I should hug her or what, and went.

It was after that visit I realized Jake and Harry should have been on that same train with Mr. Holstead. Now, like I said, a lot of folks in town might say it would be better for Skunk Corners if those two never did come back. The kind ones called them clowns, and others called them a threat to civilization, or worse.

I called them friends.

We hadn't started out that way. For a long time, they'd just been a pair of irritating and ill-bred fools. Often, they still were. But under the influence of the Ninja Librarian, I had become their teacher, and they had become young men with ideas and ambition.

Not all the ideas had been good. Their attempt to get rich selling chipmunk pelts hadn't worked out so well, and the above-mentioned Drunk Swede Mine incident was a disaster that near got them run out of town, or killed by a swarm of angry miners, or both. But they were trying, which was more than I could say of some of their elders.

Or of myself, them days.

Since the Ninja Librarian left, I had quit trying. I could see that now, looking back at the previous weeks. Maybe the storm wasn't such a bad thing. It had forced the town to work together, and it was making me think more about others than about myself.

So I tried to comfort the Holsteads, and maybe I helped, maybe I didn't. Comforting words aren't my strong point. I couldn't help thinking maybe I should find another way. Something more practical than nice words and a hug.

By morning I had plowed straight through to a simple answer.

Leaving the others to put the finishing touches on Mrs. Herberts' roof, I headed out early down the tracks. Whatever was keeping the trains from us, I'd find it, and I'd fix it if I could.

I didn't find the train that morning, but it didn't take long to figure out the problem. Every few yards, seemed like, there was a tree or branch or little slide down over the line. I'd not thought to bring a saw, but I dragged aside what I could. It took until noon for me to puzzle out what should be done, and then I turned back to do it.

Back in Skunk Corners, I rounded up half a dozen workers. That stopped progress on Tess's place, but she agreed it was more important to get the trains running, so off we went in a bunch, axes and saws over our shoulders, and a few shovels for good measure. We just lit into each and every obstruction on the track, and soon a fair number of the kids were there too, hauling away the smaller bits and cut-up pieces. They thought it was all great fun.

By night there were twice as many workers, and we'd reached the first bridge. Tess and the girls had come three times with coffee and doughnuts. The bridge looked sound, but it was too dark to continue, so we all trooped back to Skunk Corners. Tess made sure anyone who needed it got a square meal. Annie was back in her kitchen even while they rebuilt the Tavern around her, so there was good food to be had, even if we had to pass it out the window and sit outside to eat it.

Next morning we headed out at first light. The bridge was sound, and if it was a bit discomforting to cross the open ties so far above the ravine, none of us wanted to say so. Nor did we want to climb down and back up, so across we went. Enoch Johnson, who owned the mercantile, strung a rope for the nervous to hold onto.

Pretty soon, we could hear the sounds of axes echoing up the line whenever our own fell silent. We were far enough from town now that Tess and Hilda brought the big coffee pot and built a fire to brew it on the spot, but she confided to me that if the train didn't come soon, there'd be no more. And without coffee, who could work? Now we had us a real crisis.

By noon we were in sight of the train crew coming up from the other side. One more bridge lay between, and I could see it would need some repairs before you'd want to run a train across. But Johnny hopped right over, and came back a half hour later with Mr. Holstead.

Tess let go her end of the crosscut saw we shared when she wasn't cooking, and scolded him.

"You get yourself on up to home and let your wife know you're alive. She and Janey have been worried sick."

He looked at his toes, just the way my students do when I catch them misbehaving. "Aw, I know, Miz Tess. But it wouldn't have been right to just leave the train and walk home, when everyone's workin' so hard. 'Sides, we sent Jake and Harry on to let folks know we was comin', and you should start workin' down from your end." He looked around. "Where are the boys, anyway? Skipped out on the work?"

Tess and I exchanged looks. There were maybe two reasons the boys hadn't shown up, and I didn't like either one. Of course, they might have just decided to dodge work and go skylarking. That would be pretty low, but better than my other thought, which was that they'd gone and got lost or hurt on their way. Wouldn't be the first time. You'd think boys who grew up in a place like Skunk Corners could handle themselves in the woods, and up to a point they could. They could hunt and fish and even track a little. But they lacked the common sense to stay out of trouble, in town or in the woods.

I went back to town with Ike Holstead, to make sure the boys hadn't shown up meantime, and to get what I'd need for a search. While we went, he told me about getting caught by the storm halfway up the mountain. They'd been clearing the line ever since. It wasn't much damaged, but it took a lot of clearing. Then he told me everything he knew about where the boys had gone, so I had a pretty good idea where to look.

I stuffed a few extras in my pockets. Pockets are one reason I wear overalls and none of them fool dresses. At the last minute, I collected Tommy Colson and Peggy Rossiter, too. They needed something to do, and I'd have someone to send for help if need be. Besides, having company made it an outing, not just a rescue. It was a beautiful day, too nice to be grim and serious.

We headed down the mountain in a straight line for Lupine. The railroad took a big turn between there and Skunk Corners, but the boys would figure they could save time by walking a straight line. That was the way they thought—in straight lines, without any logic.

You can't walk a straight line in the woods, and they should know that. The railroad has that bend for a reason. But Jake and Harry are easily misled by excessive optimism, especially when it comes to their own abilities. They'd have hit the little cliffs about halfway and starting veering off course, always a little downhill, no doubt.

Then they'd have gotten caught by darkness. If they'd stayed put all night, they'd have gone on in the morning and have reached town in an hour or so. Since they hadn't come in, I figured they'd tried to push on, and gotten into trouble.

"Sure," Tommy said when I explained my thinking. "They'd've wanted to get to Tess's for a drink and some dinner." Two-Timin' Tess's Tavern wasn't quite itself again, but the boys wouldn't have known that. So they'd gone on and gotten stuck and by now they'd been out two nights, probably without food or water, being they weren't very beforehand about such things.

All we had to do was circle the cliffs and find out where the boys had treed themselves. Then I could figure out how to get them out. I hoped it wouldn't require a bunch of climbing. I don't mind heights, but I didn't relish hauling the boys down from some ledge. I'm big, but they're bigger, and I didn't bring any ropes.

Harry and Jake were just about where I'd expected. It didn't take us even two hours to get there, and as soon's we came around the base of those cliffs, Jake and Harry commenced hollering.

At first I couldn't figure out what was keeping them. They were perched on a ledge halfway up, sure, but in daylight it was easy enough to see the way down—or up. I could have climbed it with one hand tied behind me.

When we reached their ledge, though, we could

see the problem. The boys must've fallen, because Jake's shoulder was all funny, and Harry had sprained an ankle. They told us that Jake might've been able to help Harry if he'd had two good arms, and Harry could've helped Jake if he could've walked, but they couldn't figure a way down at all as they were.

I thought that with a little imagination they could've come up with something better than just sitting there, but I couldn't see any point in saying so. They were cold, hungry, thirsty and hurting. If they'd made bad choices, they'd had the suffering of it. And there'd be plenty of other folks with plenty to say.

I sent the kids for help. I sure wasn't lugging Harry home piggy-back, and Jake wasn't going to be much use. Once Tommy and Peggy were well on their way, I took hold of Jake's arm. Ignoring his protests, I pulled and rotated the thing until his shoulder joint just popped back into place. I'd seen my Pa do that once, on his own shoulder. They say it hurts.

Judging by Jake's language, it hurts a lot. I gave Pa a mental salute, because he hadn't said a word when he did it. Jake cussed loud and long, but I didn't learn a single new word. You'd think he'd have gotten some new vocabulary among the railroad workers.

When he was done, we tied up Harry's ankle, and I helped them down, one at a time, to wait for help.

Harry's Ma wasn't any too happy when we showed up in her yard with him on a horse Tommy'd borrowed. He and Peggy hadn't found anyone who'd help, but Yance's Pa had let them use the horse, which was enough to get us there.

I couldn't blame Mrs. Colson for not wanting another person to take care of—in addition to

Tommy and Harry, she has two sets of boy twins, ages two and three. But Harry's her son, so she had to take him until he could walk back to his job.

To my surprise, both Jake and Harry were anxious about those jobs, and Jake went right off to find the train and explain. I advised him to avoid Skunk Corners, where folks were likely a little put out that Mr. Holstead's message had gone so far astray. Then I added that he should stick to the tracks and not try anything fancy.

If looks could kill, I'd have died right there, but Jake took my advice and aimed himself at the railroad line, a ways outside of town. Maybe he figured I was right. Maybe he just wanted some distance from my kind of first aid. He was still muttering and cussing about it.

I watched until I was sure he was on the right path, then headed on to town with Peggy. Tommy stayed to help Harry, since his Ma said Harry was old enough to have known better and could take care of himself and she sure as heck wasn't going to.

In town, mostly the women were out, chopping and stacking the smaller branches that littered the street, and trying to salvage what they could of vegetable gardens and flowerbeds. Mrs. Holstead and Janey were out with little James Thomas, and greeted me with smiles and waves.

"Ike's gone back to the work crew," Mrs. Holstead called. "And Yance came back for some nails a little bit ago. He said they nearly have the trestle ready, so you needn't tramp all that way."

At that moment we heard the train whistle in the distance. Looked like Jake would be walking back up to the depot after all. I tossed a few more small bits off the tracks, just to be sure. Then I took a look up the track. Above our station, the mess of downed trees and mud resumed. I could hear no sign of any work crew from Endoline.

The station master saw my look and shrugged. "I don't reckon the train will try to continue on from here."

I didn't suppose it would. I wondered how long it would take for anyone up there to figure out what they needed to do.

Our town was a mess, but maybe Skunk Corners would make it after all. I heard cheers as the train pulled in, our work crew hanging off the platforms, and smiled. For three days we'd pulled together and done what needed doing. That was a start.

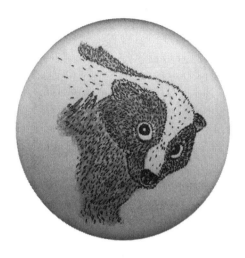

4 THE NINJA LIBRARIAN RETURNS TO SKUNK CORNERS

Skunk Corners had nearly returned to normal, or what passed for normal. There were roofs of a sort back on Mrs. Herberts' shop and old Miss Cornelia's cabin. Mr. Tolliver hadn't been seen since emerging from his uprooted outhouse, trailing a nasty aroma and turning the air blue, but smoke rose from his chimney so we knew he was alive, and no one disturbed him.

And down at Two-Timin' Tess's Tavern, the worst-hit building in town, every man who wanted a drink helped out a bit before Johnny dished him a shot from a barrel that had escaped the destruction. I don't think it was a rule or anything, they just did it.

By the end of the fourth day after the storm, most of my students were back at the school, and a framework of boards marked the new barroom over at Tess's. No one had glass in their windows;

Johnson's Mercantile had sold out what little they had in the first hour. We had to wait for another train to bring what we needed.

The wood of the fallen trees still lay in untidy heaps around town, but most was off the street, and handy for students who got a bit too rambunctious. They could split, haul or stack a goodly pile of firewood during lunch. When Hank and Yance got into a dust-up over something or other, I sent them out with a two-man crosscut saw and told them to come back when they'd cut up enough to fill the wood box. I watched from the window as they first worked against each other, too angry to cooperate, then finally decided they'd better work together, and began making progress.

Some of the more uptight townsfolk—including, of course, Mrs. Mayor Burton—thought the Tavern should remain closed. She didn't have much luck with that. Even her husband, the mayor himself, wasn't above dropping by the Tavern to hold a board in place or provide some nails—and take a drink.

I'd thought Preacher Dawson would be on Mrs. Burton's side, but he turned out to be more sensible than I would've credited.

"No, Al, I wouldn't want to see Tess's close down. The men *will* drink, and she runs a decent and honest bar. Once I thought otherwise, but I understand now."

Well! You could've knocked me down with a feather. Imagine a preacher showing common sense! And an old geezer like him admitting that he'd been wrong. I hadn't known it was possible.

I was busy morning, noon, and night. When I wasn't teaching—I'd reopened the school once we'd found the train—I was helping Tess, except when someone needed something from the library. Every single book on carpentry and the like was checked out, and several people had come looking for help making oilcloth for their windows.

The best part of it all was that I was too busy to think. I didn't have to wonder if we were a town, and Tess had promised she wasn't leaving. I might've gone on moping about Ninja Tom leaving us so sudden-like, but I'd no strength left for moping. And I couldn't lie awake worrying about the town, my students, or much of anything else, because I couldn't stay awake for even a minute after I was free to lie down.

The only thing I worried over was Billy Jenkins. Tommy had taken him home the day after the storm, but he didn't want to go. Neither did Tommy, but I insisted he and Peggy at least visit home. Even their parents would start to notice after a couple of days, and they needed clean clothes.

But the next day Billy was back, clinging to Tommy. A hand-shaped bruise discolored his left cheek.

"Mama hit me," he said when I insisted on knowing. "For not comin' home t'other night."

And Tommy, who I'd be willing to bet had been socked a time or two himself, bristled indignantly.

"She was that mad, and that drunk, so when she hit him I just grabbed hold and took 'im home with me. An' he's not goin' back there, not without Jake nohow." Tommy seemed sure that Jake could protect Billy, though I wasn't so sure. Jake didn't head my list of responsible folks. Anyway, Jake would be keeping shy of Skunk Corners for a while, even when his job didn't have him elsewhere.

"Your ma'll keep him?" I asked Tommy.

He scuffed a toe in the dirt. "Well, she was a-mighty nice about it last night."

"But," I prompted. I was pretty sure where this was going to end up.

"But she tol' me this mornin' that she's her hands

full with her own little 'uns, and no way she could take on another youngster."

Tommy, I knew, had four little brothers, two sets of twins just two and three years old. I could see his mother's point. It was also why Tommy ran so wild, to avoid going home any more than he had to. Between the work he might end up having to do if he were around, and the irritations that came of just being around the twins, he'd want to stay away.

But what to do with Billy? The boy had run off to play with the town kids, trusting me to make things good. I felt the responsibility like a two-ton weight. The children expected me to make everything all right. They thought I really knew stuff.

If Jake came back, maybe he could control Ina Jenkins, which would be good for her and good for Billy. I wasn't so sure it'd be good for Jake. Anyway, he wasn't here now, and Billy was. As for Billy's father, I didn't know where he was or if he'd be any use if we could find him.

"I thought maybe Billy could stay with you," Tommy said.

That's how I'd come to have Billy Jenkins sharing my quarters, and on my exhausted mind. I'd felt bad, leaving him to roam loose whilst I worked, first on the town and then on the tracks, but Eunice and MaryBeth had taken him under their wings and told me to do what needed doing.

Now I was taking advice from ten-year-olds.

When I came to her with my worry, Tess said Billy could come stay with her, once she had a place again, which would be soon at the rate we were going. For now, she and the girls were still living in Tom's old quarters at the library. Johnny camped in the relatively undamaged kitchen of Two-Timin' Tess's Tavern, just to keep an eye on things. Besides, his usual bunk was in the shed out back, which had been flattened by a fallen tree.

So you'd think I'd not have much to worry about, with Tess backing me, but I worried anyway. I didn't know how long it'd be before Billy's mother sobered up enough to come looking for him, and I didn't think I had much of a leg to stand on, keeping him from her. But I wasn't sending him back. Not unless his Pa came home, and then only if he showed he'd do right by the boy.

Meanwhile, I fretted over Billy's immediate needs. He'd nothing but the clothes he stood in, and I had little enough to spare, and none of it any use to him. Worse, he needed a mother, not a school teacher who didn't know what she was doing. Well, maybe Tess and the girls would make family enough, once he moved in with them.

I went to Miss Cornelia for help with clothing, since she'd done well by us in the matter of winter coats. She rounded up a few things, and made no comment. I couldn't tell if she thought I was doing a good thing or not. Maybe she didn't know, any more than I did.

I even thought of asking Preacher Dawson, which shows just how confused I was by this new responsibility. That, and his unexpected behavior with regard to Tess's Tavern. I'd even seen him helping out at Tess's, though not drinking. Maybe the old fellow was lonely. The tavern always had got more business than the church.

None of this worried Billy at all. He was eating three times a day, probably for the first time in his life, and if my cooking left a great deal to be desired, it beat going hungry. Besides, Annie helped us both out a fair bit, so we weren't doing that badly. She was back in her kitchen and feeding all comers. Billy did little chores around the school and library, and trotted after Tommy or me wherever he could, apparently content.

About the only sensible thing I did about then was go back to practicing what Tom had taught me. The exercise helped me sleep, and I had a feeling I might need those skills, fresh and sharp, not dull and neglected. Tom might have left me without finishing the job, but I had no excuse for not using what he'd taught me.

By the time the tracks were clear and the train could reach town, I'd begun wondering if Billy's ma was going to just let him go, like an unwanted kitten. Another part of me fretted that maybe she'd drunk herself to death. Either notion bothered me so much that I was almost relieved when I finally saw Ina Jenkins forging her unsteady way up the road to the school.

If I was relieved, why did my stomach feel so odd?

Matters didn't improve when Billy, standing next to me, tip-toed to peer out the window and said,

"Uh-oh. She brought Uncle Cal with her."

And why hadn't I known that Ina was sister to Cal Potts, a low-down trouble-maker from Two-Bit? Anyway, I thought he'd been locked up for trying to rob our bank last Halloween. Seemed he'd wormed his way out one way or another, and probably wasn't too happy with me for my part in getting him locked up.

Thinking about what might come, I made a quick decision.

"Tommy, you and Peg keep all the children in and bar the door behind me. No one is taking Billy away," I added, on account of not wanting him to look so scared. MaryBeth took his hand, and all the children closed in around him.

I stepped out into the street to face down trouble. I heard the bar thud into place behind me. Tommy and Peg take their duties seriously.

I moved away from the school and hoped Tom

had taught me enough for this.

Ina Jenkins looked me up and down when she reached the school, and spat.

Cal Potts stood there looking mean.

"I want my boy," she announced.

Cal practiced making fists.

"He doesn't want you," I told her flat out. Cal I pretended to ignore, though I was keeping an eye on him.

"Don't matter. He's my boy. I could have the law on you."

"I don't like folks who hit children. I say he stays here."

"He's my boy." She sure could stick to an idea, even if she couldn't walk a straight line. "I've a right to dish—dis'pline him."

"No one has the right to hit a child in the face hard enough to leave a bruise."

Cal cracked his knuckles. Ina spat again to show her contempt for my notions.

"Reckon yer the only one'd say so."

A voice spoke from behind me. "So say we all."

I didn't have to turn to know it was Tess. I didn't know who was with her but that could wait. I wasn't taking my eyes off Cal Potts. He must've figured I'd be distracted, though, because he jumped right at me. Or maybe he just didn't think I could fight him.

He was wrong.

Before I knew what was happening, I had twisted, lifted, and sent him flying over my hip into the dirt, as neatly as the Ninja Librarian could have done. I'd practiced so much, I didn't need to think. I turned back in time to give Ina a shove with my foot that sent her sprawling in the road. She was still drunk and in no shape to fight, so that was enough to keep her out of it.

I had to knock Cal down a few more times, but

eventually he got the idea and stayed down. Only then did I turn to thank Tess for backing me, and got a shock that near laid me out alongside Cal.

After a moment, I reached up and shut my jaw with my own hand. There beside Tess stood the Ninja Librarian.

Tom.

In my shock, I didn't even notice the other townsfolk standing with them, but my opponents did. As soon as they could find their feet, Ina and Cal took off back where they'd come from. When they were gone, Tess and the others headed back to work.

Then we two were alone on the street, and I still hadn't spoken. At last Tom broke the silence.

"I came back to see if you needed me."

Needed him? "Do we need you?" I thought about the last few weeks. About all the things we'd done poorly, and what we'd done anyway, even without knowing how.

I shook my head. "No."

Tom's eyebrows went up, and I freed my tongue.

"We've survived a storm that destroyed half of Skunk Corners, rebuilt our town and the Tavern, mostly anyhow, cleared the line for the train to come through, and I can keep the scum in line." I gestured at the departing Pottses.

"So no, I don't reckon we do need you." I was nearly shouting now, and he half turned away, like maybe he was leaving, and I didn't even know if I'd stop him.

Then my voice caught in my throat, so Tom could hardly hear me. "But we missed you something fierce."

And that seemed to answer his question, because he picked up his little valise and headed for the library.

I decided not to warn him what he'd find there.

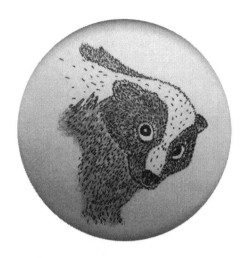

5 THE NINJA LIBRARIAN SETTLES IN

I watched the Ninja Librarian walk into the library, and a whole load of odd sensations ran through me like squirrels up a tree.

I was still mad at him.

I was happy he was back.

I really wanted to see how he'd react to the women's laundry drying in his kitchen.

That last notion won, and I trotted across the street after him. The girls were all at the Tavern, dividing their energies between feeding people and driving nails. The library was empty of people but full up with evidence they were living there.

That fact apparently struck Tom as soon as he opened the door. Before he could possibly have seen anything out of order, I saw him hesitate and raise his head a little, as though sniffing. Coming up behind him, I could tell why. Annie had evidently left a pot of soup simmering on the back of the stove, and the aroma was something to conjure with.

Tom glanced at me—I was too close now to
escape his notice—and went on in. I followed hard
on his heels. I wouldn't miss this for anything.

Much to my disappointment, I supposed thanks
to the soup, Tom showed no surprise when he
opened the door to his rooms.

Laundry was draped about the kitchen—the
private sort you couldn't put on a clothes line, at
least not right in town. A couple of corn-shuck
mattresses lay in the corner, since his sleeping
quarters weren't big enough for all five women. And
some indefinably female smell could be detected
lurking behind the scent of that soup. Perfume, or
soap, or something. I'd smelled that same thing once
when I went upstairs in the Tavern, where the men
couldn't go. My quarters didn't have it.

Tom ignored all that. He set his valise just outside
the door, crossed to the stove, and lifted the lid of the
soup pot. Then he filled a bowl and cleared a space
to sit down at the table. Trying not to look at what
he held, he moved some undergarments off a chair,
and sat down, spoon in hand.

Only when he had gulped half the soup did he
acknowledge my presence.

"It appears," he observed, "that I shall require
other accommodations for the time being."

"Unless you want to share with Tess, Tildy, Hilda,
Julia and Annie."

He looked around the room, which felt crowded
even without the girls actually present. His gaze
jumped over the unmentionables hanging on a line
near the stove.

"I think not."

He might've been waiting for me to offer a
suggestion, but I wouldn't. Whether he knew it or
not, I hadn't forgiven our Ninja Librarian. I let him
figure it out for himself. He could sleep out in the
library itself, though I supposed people would still

talk. Or—

"Where is Johnny staying?"

Darn him, seeing answers so fast I could hardly think up the questions!

"In Tess's kitchen."

"I shall ask if I might join him, I believe." He turned back to his bowl. "When I have finished this excellent soup."

I watched him in wonder. I had never seen Tom eat so much or so fast, not even at the amazing Fourth of July picnic last summer. He'd been cool and restrained then, unlike me. I considered getting a bowl for myself, but I wasn't ready to sit down at table with him. I would get some later.

After a bit he noticed me watching, and I swear he looked embarrassed. Like shoveling in Annie's good soup might be a crime. You ask me, as good a cook as she is, *not* to gulp it down might be a bigger crime.

"It has been a day or two since I have had a meal," Tom explained.

I didn't know what to say about that, so I muttered something about having work to do and left.

I could always find work, as much as I wanted. A few minutes with a hammer and nails left me feeling much more like myself.

Later, I saw Tom come out of the library and make his way up the street to Two-Timin' Tess's Tavern. I was on the roof—we'd started in on that the day before. I like working on roofs. You see a lot, and since people hardly ever look up, most of the time they don't know you're there.

I wasn't surprised that Tom looked up. He's one of the few who *do* notice everything, even what's over their heads. When he lifted a hand, I gave a guarded nod. I still didn't know how I felt about him coming back. I only knew how I felt about him leaving.

Seemed like I wasn't the only one. As he passed among the denizens of Skunk Corners, Tom's greetings were met by nods or, at best, a brief "good day." A few people just looked.

I watched it all. Tom's face remained unreadable, but I thought I knew what was going on. He had expected we'd all greet him happily and things would be just the same again.

Well, he'd left us and let us down and we weren't ready to pretend it never happened. Maybe he was seeing that. And that made me curious enough to slide down from the roof and watch Tom's encounter with Johnny. How would Tess's barkeep respond to a request to share his sleeping space?

Johnny, apparently, didn't mind. I halted outside the bar in time to hear him say,

"Sure. Plenty of room. You want to stow your bag behind the bar until closing?" Now that the walls were up and the roof nearly done, Johnny had moved his whiskey—or whatever it was—back inside.

I peered in and the two men looked comfortable as Johnny tucked Tom's valise away before going back to work. Did Johnny know something I didn't? Or did he just figure it was too much work to hold a grudge?

Tom looked around, taking in the construction and the mess it had made. After a long study, he took up a broom and began sweeping.

Well. That was a point in his favor.

I went off to the kitchen to find out what Tess thought of it all.

When I finished telling Tess all I'd seen, she just looked at me.

"Al, do you really have to ask?"

Well, maybe I'm slow, but if I'd understood, I wouldn't have asked. Still, I made a stab at it.

"Folks don't know what to think." That was easy. *I* didn't know what to think. "What do you think, Tess? Why'd he come back?"

Just to complete my aggravation and frustration, Tess shrugged. She wouldn't say anything more.

I gave up and went back to the roof. Shingles I understood. People were a lot tougher.

I kept my distance from everyone the rest of the afternoon, but come dinnertime there was no help for it. When Billy came and hollered for me, I had to climb down. MaryBeth had gone home, and I didn't want Billy left alone anywhere until I could be sure he wouldn't be grabbed by his mother or the low-down Cal Potts.

When I got down, Billy grabbed me by the hand and pulled me into the newly-roofed Tavern.

"Teacher! He's back! Mister Tom came back!"

"I know." I recollected Billy was only six, and made my tone a little nicer. "I saw him earlier."

"Well, come *on*. I wanta say hey."

Looked like there was one resident of Skunk Corners who didn't have any doubts. I guessed Billy was just glad someone had come back.

I felt a little bad I'd pushed Jake off back to the trains so fast, but he and Harry need their railroad jobs—and Skunk Corners still wasn't a real safe place for them.

Tom traded his broom for a dish of venison stew, and sat at the kitchen table between Johnny and Hilda. Everyone ate like eating was all that was on their minds.

Annie handed Billy and me our own bowls of stew, and we sat down. When I'd taken the edge off my appetite, I jumped right in with both feet.

"Well? Why'd you come back?"

"An' why'd you leave us?" Billy put in, asking what I wasn't sure I dared.

Tom looked at us, then around the table.

"Much as I'm tempted to point out that it really is my own business, I think you deserve an answer." He glanced around the kitchen again. Everyone was watching him, and faces were guarded, not letting feelings out—which told a lot about our feelings, now that I think of it.

"I left because my work here was done."

"You mean because we handled those toughs on our own, and without any blood spilled, either?" I asked.

He nodded. "In part. And you got the school working, and well, you were a *town*. You *are* a town. You said it yourself, Alice. You don't need me."

"So why did you come back, if we don't need you?" I tried hard to be calm and cool, but to me it sounded like I was whining. Or hunting a fight.

Tom didn't rise to my bait. "Isn't it enough that I did come back?"

"I think you know that it is not," Tess said.

"It will have to do." For once, Tom did not ask his customary "does that completely answer your question?" Nor would he say anything more.

Over the next few days, I kept my distance from Tom, and he kept himself busy. Everywhere I looked, seemed like, I saw the Ninja Librarian helping someone. And Billy stopped shadowing me and Tommy, and went to following Tom around, fetching him tools and drinks of water.

If at first people greeted Tom warily, by the end of the second day they were thawing. He was really good at doing just about everything, and his plan might have been obvious, but it was working. Billy's devotion to him probably helped, too. Pretty soon, Tess and I were the only ones who still seemed wary. Maybe that made sense, because we were the ones who'd been most hurt by him leaving without a word. He was supposed to be our friend.

In a funny way, Tom had the same problem I'd had when Janey Holstead and her Ma were so worried about Mr. Holstead. He didn't know how to fix feelings and fears, however smart he was about other things.

That actually made me feel some better, and more inclined to like him again. Tom was smart, no question about it. When we couldn't make the windows fit on the new barroom, he created a plumb-bob and a level from a string, some lead, and a bowl of water, and got us to fuss with it until our walls were plumb, level, and true.

But he didn't come looking to talk to me, and he didn't tell me to come start my Ninja-fighter lessons again, so I figured he didn't know what to say to me, no more than I knew what to say to him. We sat at opposite ends of the table, dinnertimes, and I don't think I said more than "pass the salt" for three days.

Finally, about the time we finished the repairs on Two-Timin' Tess's Tavern, I saw Tess approach him. Even if it was just to say she and the girls were moving back to the Tavern, she seemed to have thawed considerably.

I could see what he was doing. He'd made himself useful and pleasant, and people decided to forgive him. But I still wanted to know why he'd come back. And who said he had to leave, just because we'd learned to, well, take care of ourselves? And what was to stop him from leaving again, just as suddenly? No, I wasn't ready to trust him just yet.

It took a week, a week of the two of us stepping carefully around each other, but in the end, I had to do it.

"Okay. You're back, and I can see you want us all to know you're helping us and all that. But I still have to know. Why?"

I caught a glimpse of Tess's skirt around the

corner. We were out by the woodshed, where Annie'd sent us both to get firewood. Well, if Tess wanted to listen, I wouldn't rat on her. She needed an answer too.

It took Tom a long time to get his stack of wood just the way he wanted it. I'd about decided he wasn't going to answer, and had turned to go when he finally spoke.

"I came back because I missed this place."

That had to be a lie.

"You missed Skunk Corners? This gawd-forsaken dust heap?"

"Yes." I guess my face expressed my disbelief, because he thought some more, then said, "Perhaps not the place so much, though I do find the area attractive. But the town isn't this lot of buildings, Alice."

I waited.

"I came back because I missed you people. You, and Tess and the girls, and the children." He gave me a look that might've been a glare.

"Does that completely answer your question?"

Did it? I had no idea.

Tom did, though. "And," he added to finish convincing me, "because you need more lessons. Starting as soon as we have this wood hauled in. Your form when you fought Mr. Potts was appallingly sloppy."

Well, *that* answered my question, alright.

6 THE NINJA LIBRARIAN TAKES HOLD

I had thought it would take the Ninja Librarian a while to get his feet under him and get back to business as usual, but he set me straight pretty quick.

Not that he said anything. He did it before I was even speaking to him. Just as soon as the Tavern was back together enough for the girls to move back in—and out of his quarters—Tom had the library open. It being Thursday, he'd opened up for Story Time. Suspicious of him or not, the young mothers wanted his stories, given what a lousy job I'd been doing, and they came in droves.

Then he closed down again. I could see from the school that he'd closed the shutters and gone off to the Tavern. I didn't figure he'd gone for a drink.

In fact, I don't think I ever did see him drink anything stronger than Johnny's coffee—which might be stronger than a lot of what Mrs. Mayor Burton calls Strong Drink. Johnny says it keeps his hair curly, but I think it just peels the enamel off my teeth. I go to Annie when I want coffee.

Anyway, Tom must've gone to help out at Tess's, which was the only place in town not back to itself again. Window glass had come in on the next train after he did, and pretty nearly everyone had fixed their broken windows. Hank and Yance had spent the morning repairing those in the school, rather than doing sums and learning history.

Honestly, it was a better use of their time. I still couldn't get those two through the Sixth Reader, and as for figures and history, they couldn't see the point at all, so no amount of teaching on my part sank in. They thought they were trying, but with their hearts not in it, the effort never took hold.

The Ninja Librarian had taught me that: a wishfulness to learn is more than half the battle. That'd been what made Crazy Jake and Wild Harry take to reading—and then to math, when they'd needed to know figures, too—after years of scorning books as being for sissies who didn't know how to fight.

Of course, the steam boiler they'd helped build had blown up before it could heat a drop of water, but the process had led to those railroad jobs they were now trying so hard to keep. Tommy told me Harry had ridden into town and caught the midnight train to go back to work, just as soon as he could limp to the barn and saddle the horse.

As I said, Tom went off after Story Time to help Tess out. They were putting the finishing touches on the new barroom—and repairing what tables and chairs could be fixed.

I know, because I went over at lunch, and found Tom painstakingly fitting the rungs back into a chair, a pot of glue beside him.

We hadn't really made up yet, but he looked up when I approached and spoke to me anyway.

"Alice. Just hold this in place while I clamp it,

would you please?"

I wondered how he'd clamp something so big, but he'd already thought of that. A few loops of twine and a knot I couldn't quite make out, and it was tight as could be.

Tom took up the next chair, and began rummaging for the right bits to repair it.

Next day he did the same thing, and this time when I came along, we'd made up, at least sort of. And I'd had my first fighting lesson in a long time, because when Tom had said I needed more lessons "starting now," he'd not been kidding. We'd delivered the firewood and gone back to the library basement for a painful hour of drills and kicks.

Now when he asked me to fetch him a bit of broken chair from the far side of the pile, I could have groaned. Maybe I did, a little, because he asked ever so innocently,

"Are you a trifle sore today, Alice?"

I'd have liked to have lied, but it never has done me any good, lying to Tom. He always knows.

"Maybe a little." At least a little in every muscle there was, and maybe some others, too.

"Did you practice while I was away?" This was treading on thin ice. I wasn't sure I'd completely forgiven him for leaving, and didn't want him prying into how I'd taken it.

"Of course I did!"

He saw through that as well.

"Just not as much as you meant to, perhaps?"

Well, that was the limit! Annie might've got us to speaking again, but I wasn't over my hurt. I stood up, stiff in both body and manner. "I have to return to my class."

He was right, of course. But he didn't have to say it.

When I let school out that day, Ninja Tom was back in the library, and the children nearly all made a bee-line for the place. I followed more slowly, curious. I noticed Hank and Yance took off for home, but all the others charged in, and their interest seemed to be about equally in Tom and in his books.

He'd brought new ones, though I'd not seen him with more than that little valise, so I don't know how.

I stood on the doorstep a moment, looking from Peg and Tommy, who fell on the books like vultures on lion kill, to my other Sixth Reader pupils, hurrying off to—what? Maybe farm work for their folks, maybe just some fishin'. I did wish I could reach those two somehow.

Then I went on in. Maybe he'd brought something for me, too. I could use some new reads.

Turned out he'd brought me a pair of story books by a man named Mark Twain, and a set of books on advanced mathematics. I looked at those curiously. "Advanced Algebraic Studies" "Trigonometry" "An Introduction to the Calculus." I didn't even know what those last two were, though at least I knew about Algebra. Advanced Algebra sounded like work. I stole a look at the librarian. Were these for me to learn, or was I going to have to teach these subjects I'd never heard of?

"Tom?" I held up the books in question, and he crossed the room to me, followed by Tommy and Peggy, who'd seen the exchange. He knew what I was asking.

"I believe you will have need of those. I suggest you begin on them soon."

The children had taken the books, and were looking through them, Peg with more interest than Tommy. She's good at math, that girl.

"I think Tommy and I could do this stuff pretty soon." She held up the Advanced Algebra book.

That was probably true. They'd pretty nearly finished the geometry book. I looked at the books and sighed. It's not that I don't like math—I do, though not so well as history. But I'm awful busy these days.

So, without really thinking about it, we fell back into the old routines: school, books, my lessons. With Tess's place finished, Billy moved in with the girls. After having one mama who neglected him, he now had five who, I think, loved him. They certainly took good care of him.

I could see why Mr. Jenkins would've left that worthless spawn of Two-Bit he'd for some reason married. What on earth had possessed the man? Jake was flea-brained, but I couldn't see him doing something so stupid as marrying into the Potts family. In any case, however vile his wife, I did not see how Jenkins could have left his boy.

Those worries got pushed to the back of my mind, with Billy out of my room. I was more concerned about Hank and Yance.

In the end, I did what I might as well have done in the beginning: I took the problem to the Ninja Librarian. I laid it all out for him.

"So, I don't know if I'm supposed to do more to teach those two, or just give up and let them go, like Susanna."

Susanna Calloway had quit school the year before, at seventeen, without ever finishing the Sixth Reader or mastering long division. She was married now, and if my eyes weren't lying, she'd soon be joining the young mamas at Story Time. It seemed like no kind of life to me, though she looked happy. So far.

Were Hank and Yance meant to just work the farm? Was that what they wanted?

Tom thought about my problem. He knew the

boys, of course. I could tell after a minute that he didn't have the answer any more than I did.

In the end, I came up with all the wisdom we could muster between us:

"Maybe I should just ask them what they want?"

So the next day when school let out and all the other children trooped over to the library, I stopped Hank and Yance. I perched myself on the desk next to theirs and looked them over, and they tried not to look guilty. So far's I knew, they hadn't done anything lately to be guilty over. It's just that being kept after made them sure they were in some kind of trouble. That's the worst of being the teacher. I can hardly talk to a kid without getting them all worried, at least inside the schoolhouse.

Eventually I found some words and put the boys out of their misery.

"Do you two know what you want to do with yourselves? For your future, I mean." Well, that was a big, hard question for them. They thought a bit.

"Work the farm, I guess?" It came out of Yance like a question.

"You like it?"

"Naw, not really." Hank seemed more confident than his brother. "But what else is there to do?"

"I don't think we're smart enough to do like Jake and Harry," his twin opined. "I mean, here we are gonna be eighteen next month and we can't even get through the Sixth Reader. Or fractions."

"Jake and Harry couldn't either," I pointed out. "Not until they decided they needed to."

"Yeah, but we've really tried, Teacher. We know you feel bad about us." The boys looked so discouraged I didn't know what to say. I thought maybe that was part of the trouble, though. They'd been trying for me, not for themselves. To avoid looking at them, I let my gaze roam the room, over to the window.

The window.

The window they'd glazed so well, as well as any man in town.

I looked back at them, and only knew enough not to blurt it all out when I didn't have a real plan yet.

"I think I have an idea, boys." They looked at me like a pair of lost puppies who smelled home. I wondered uneasily if they knew I was no font of wisdom, just a tomboy only a little older than they were.

I nodded at the window. "Did you enjoy doing that? And building the boiler?"

"Sure," Hank said. "Makin' stuff, that's fun. But we can't think it through, seems like."

"Well, you let me think a bit. Maybe I have an idea."

I took my idea to Tom that night after dinner.

"I think I know what's between working the farm and using book learning."

"Oh?"

"Craftsmanship. Hank and Yance have some skill, I think. Maybe carpentry, or woodworking, not the part that needs math, but the kind that needs a feel for the job." I looked at him. "Like the way you fixed those chairs."

Tom, in his turn, asked for time to think. In the meantime, he put my loudly griping muscles through another workout, to remind me that, as he says, daily practice is essential to any undertaking.

Next day, Tom and I both cornered the boys after school. I wasted no time getting to the point. I wasn't sure how they'd take it.

"You two are wasting your time here."

Both boys groaned. "Aw, Teacher, if'n we drop out, Pa'll have us clearing land dawn to dark."

"Which," I told them, "would make better use of your time than setting here staring blankly at your books."

"Yeah, but." Their faces were so long they near touched the floor.

Tom took pity on them, and me. "What Miss Alice is saying is that we have a plan that will keep you in school, yet make better use of the time." He outlined the shape of their new days: mornings spent in school learning what they needed to know for the afternoons they'd spend working with various townsfolk, learning carpentry and craft until they knew what they were meant to do.

I had been surprised when Tom had offered himself, not to teach them about libraries—which would be a waste of effort—or fighting, but about woodworking.

Starting with the furniture from Tess's.

"And when that's done, we'll move you on to some real carpentry." Tom looked at the boys with a glimmer of his old self, a glimmer I only now realized had been missing.

"Does that completely answer your question?"

7 THE NINJA LIBRARIAN HEATS UP

Skunk Corners was running smoothly once again.
With Hank and Yance productively employed at
last, I was free to concentrate on bringing along my
younger pupils—and on frantically learning Algebra,
while Tommy and Peggy raced to the end of the
Geometry book. I was in trouble and I knew it.

At least I could teach Janey Holstead what she
needed to know to move up to the Sixth Reader and
basic Algebra. Her classmate, MaryBeth Burton,
stayed stolidly in the midst of her Fifth Reader, and
showed no sign yet of mastering the multiplication
and division of fractions. I wasn't sure she cared,
either.

MaryBeth did enjoy reading stories, though.
When I ran out of other options, I set her to reading
to Billy and little Melly, who were working hard to
master their ABCs.

My other students ranged through the readers,
each at his or her own pace. The result in the

schoolroom was a sort of organized chaos. It only occasionally drove me crazy. Those times, I'd declare a "nature study day" and we'd spend the afternoon down at the creek or up on the mountain, studying bugs and birds and how water flows. The sounds of the woods would calm us all, and we'd be ready to study again the next day.

It was after one of those afternoons out that I came back to the school and found Tom contemplating the windmill-driven water system he'd helped create the previous winter.

"It's working very well," I assured him. I didn't know just what he was up to, but I was certain it was something. He wore that look—bland as porridge without salt—that told me he had something to hide.

Ninja Librarians aren't as different from school children as they think.

"I am glad we were able to spare the children the trips to the spring," Tom said.

"Are you thinking of running it on over to the library?"

"It would be an interesting project."

I saw what he was doing. He was looking for construction projects for Hank and Yance. They'd nearly finished with Tess's furniture.

The next week, I found Tom down by the train depot, contemplating the steam engine that stood puffing and hissing on the track that led to Endoline.

I began to have a nasty hunch that he had more on his mind than piping water to the library.

When I saw Hank and Yance with him at the depot two days later, I was sure. Tom was thinking about hot water again, and I had to do something to stop him. This time he might make a real disaster.

"No," I said. "You will not build another boiler and blow up my school again."

Tom turned, trying to pretend he wasn't startled,

and the boys took off like the guilty rascals they doubtless were.

Tom raised an eyebrow. "Alice. How nice to see you."

"I said—" I began.

"I know what you said. I assure you, we have no plans for further explosions."

I noticed that he didn't say they wouldn't be building any steam devices. We hadn't planned on explosions the last time, either.

Tom prevented me from pursuing the matter. With a glance at the sun, he said,

"I perceive it is time for your lesson, Alice. I will see you at the library in five minutes."

Since I know better than to be late to a lesson, even if he just made up the appointment on the spot, I left in a hurry. I knew what he'd done, and why, but I had no idea what to do about it.

All I could do was keep a close eye on all three of those gents for the next several days. Hank and Yance applied themselves diligently to fractions, explaining that carpenters needed to be able to figure all sorts of measurements. That was good news, because they really did seem to learn better, knowing how they would use the knowledge. That made me think, too.

I only caught them at the depot once, but who knew what they were up to with Tom while I was still in class with the younger children? I could only be sure nothing was being built behind the school, which was some relief.

About then I developed another problem. Peggy insisted that she and Tommy should start the Advanced Algebra book, and I couldn't deny them. They'd finished the Geometry book, and I couldn't stump them on any part of it. Problem was, we had only one book for the three of us, and I had only reached the second chapter myself, so I couldn't let them take it home. I needed to keep studying it to stay ahead.

Being a little annoyed still with Tom, I took my problem to Mr. Mayor Burton. It was a school problem, after all, and he was supposed to be the head of the School Board as well as mayor. I didn't really believe the Board existed, since they'd held no meetings that I knew of since appointing me teacher, and maybe none before, either. But I thought I should try.

Mayor Burton gave me the brush-off, which I might have expected.

"Miss, we have no funds for such matters."

I ground my teeth at being called "Miss." "Al" was good enough for nearly everyone else around Skunk Corners, so why did he have to be that way? Still, I kept my temper.

"We need those books so I can keep teaching the more advanced students." I tried to keep my tone polite, but the best I could manage was cool.

"Nonsense. The Sixth Reader and Woolley's Geometry were good enough for me, and they are good enough for the children you have now."

"Even MaryBeth?" I asked. I knew there wasn't the slightest chance MaryBeth would be needing advanced Algebra books, or even geometry. But the mayor probably didn't.

"MaryBeth? MaryBeth is a girl and has no need of advanced studies. Girls' brains are not suited to such matters in any case."

That made me so mad I couldn't decide if I was more insulted by his insult to female smarts or amused by his apparently having forgotten already that I was a member of the despised and supposedly incapable sex.

Or maybe he hadn't. Maybe he thought I couldn't teach higher mathematics.

Maybe he didn't even know what Algebra was, said a part of my mind that couldn't seem to muster much respect for my elders.

And maybe I should let him try to explain to Peggy why she couldn't possibly understand the math she inhaled. The thought of what Peg would say to the slower-witted mayor made me smile. MaryBeth comes by her weak intellect honestly, though I have no idea how she ended up so sweet-natured.

None of that helped my problem. I'd have to go to Tom after all. I wondered if I could afford to buy my own copy of the book. Buying meals at Tess's used up most of the five dollars the town paid me each month, when they remembered.

Fortunately, Tom proved willing to, as he put it, "acquire an additional copy" of the Algebra text. Tommy and Peggy could share, and I could keep working to stay a few pages ahead of them.

Later, I would wonder if Tom had been so eager to help me just to keep me too busy to see what he was up to. Certainly my new studies were very absorbing. Along about then, too, Janey announced that she wanted to study more history—what our books had to say about the age of knights in armor was just enough to make her curious, but not enough to satisfy. So I launched into extra reading for her sake, finding books she could study and learning more so we could talk about them.

All that might explain why I never noticed that Tom had the boys down at the depot every afternoon, and that they were building something. They must've roped in Tommy and Peggy too, else those two would have told me, if only to get square for being left out.

Instead, I learned about the whole thing from Wild Harry Colson and Crazy Jake Jenkins. Harry had managed to limp back to work on the railroad two weeks after I'd dragged him out of the woods with a sprained ankle, but he and Jake were still keeping a low profile around town.

Only, they needed help sometimes with the paperwork they had to do. So they'd get off the night train when it came through Skunk Corners, and come hammer on my door until I got up and opened the schoolroom.

Heaven only knows what people would've said if anyone saw them. Lucky for whatever reputation I had, the boys were most interested in not being seen, just in case folks still held a grudge over one indiscretion or another. Anyway, the only folks awake at that hour were at Tess's and probably not seeing so straight.

Some might've thought I'd fallen in love with one or the other of those boys, they being about the only eligible bachelors in Skunk Corners anywhere near my age. But I was having none of it, and they seemed too much in awe of my brains, which looked a lot bigger from where they stood, to think of courtship. It was my brains they wanted, and that suited me just fine. I was no more interested in courting them than I had been in Nebuchadnezzar Jones. I'd kicked him out of town. First with my left foot, then with my right.

Anyway, one night when they came for help, Jake asked,

"Say, Al, whatever does Mr. Tom have Hank and Yance doing? I see him and them twins down at the tracks all the time. I thought they was learning carpentry."

"Uh huh," Harry corroborated. "They're building something, I reckon. And keeping it well hid, too."

Well. Carpentry was building things, but they wouldn't be doing that down by the tracks. I knew of one thing Tom had on his mind, so it was an easy guess, in a general way. But what on earth could he do clear over by the depot that would get hot water to the library?

And, if it might work, had I cut myself out of it by complaining about them blowing things up?

Naturally, I had to find out. Next afternoon when I dismissed school I headed right on over to the tracks, not stopping to mark papers or even put them away.

I was in time to see Tommy and Peggy disappear into the brush across from the depot, and knew I'd been right about them.

In fact, when I came through the brush and found where they were working, the only person missing was Tom himself.

The kids all turned when I cleared my throat. Then we stood looking at each other as I realized I had no idea what I wanted to say. Was I going to bawl them out for working on a project Tom dreamed up? Yell at them for putting their learning and skills to use? I cleared my throat.

"Erm. Whatcha all making here?"

Peggy rolled her eyes. "Teacher, you don't do that very well."

I wasn't sure what she meant by "that" but I supposed it had something to do with my effort to sound like I'd just happened on them. Fine. I wouldn't pretend.

"What in tarnation are you all up to? And where's Mr. Tom?"

"He'll be along," Tommy piped up. "We don't need him much anymore."

"He wanted us to figure it out ourselves," Yance explained. "He said we'd learn more that way."

That sounded like the Ninja Librarian, all right. But—

"Figure out what?" I still didn't trust them.

Hank pointed to a weird device, which I'd taken

for a pile of scraps and pipes.

"We're going to harvest some heat from the trains," he said, as though it explained everything.

"Harvest—how, and what for?" I crossed my arms and waited for an answer.

Peg rolled her eyes again. "You know, Teacher. How the trains pull in and puff and shoot off steam and all?"

I nodded.

"So we'll capture that heat and use it to warm water for Mr. Tom's bath."

I had to sit down. Fortunately, there was a fallen tree handy, so I didn't go all the way to the ground. Their idea came so close to working.

"Is he going to run out here to bathe when the train comes in?"

They just looked at me. I tried again. "How will you get the warm water from here to the library? Even if you manage to heat some—and you know the train only comes here at noon and midnight— how could you get it all the way over to the library without it getting cold again?"

Tom had come up behind me while I spoke. I'd felt his presence, and now I swear I could hear his face fall. The kids all looked glum, too.

They looked from me to Tom and back to their machine several times. Then Tommy sighed.

"Well," and his tone was the funereal one he'd used to announce we were out of cookies at lunch, "*that's* a question."

And how had the Ninja Librarian failed to see that flaw?

No one offered any answers.

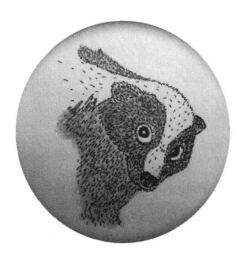

8 THE NINJA LIBRARIAN AND THE SKUNK CORNERS SKUNK

Summer had hold of Skunk Corners again, and I was thinking about dismissing school for the season. It was June, and we'd hit a hot spell that made the schoolroom near unbearable, even with all the doors and windows open.

It made me wonder if Tom was still hankering for hot water. Me, I was happy to head for the creek and the deep cool pools there. I knew it'd be a lot hotter before it was cooler, but that first hot spell each year always melts me. Later on I get a little used to it.

Funny thing was, my students didn't seem to want me to close the school. Other years, soon's it got a bit warm in May, they'd be saying it must be time to shut down. This year, no one said anything, and I thought maybe we should just keep going.

But the town doesn't pay me for July and August. Besides, I knew the school house would soon be too hot for anything, even for kids who for some reason suddenly wanted to learn.

In the end, I picked a day and announced we'd be starting the summer recess the next week. It had gotten hot enough that no one protested much. It was just too miserable indoors. But I worried what some of the kids would get up to with no school to keep them busy.

For one thing, Peggy pestered me until I let her take home the Advanced Algebra book. I knew what that meant. By the time I reopened the school in the fall, she'd be ready to teach it to Tommy and me. I gave that some thought. Maybe she could teach Tommy and let me off. I could surely use the time to help the others. But part of me hated the idea of not keeping up with a twelve-year-old.

And part of me just wanted to know the stuff, even if I do like history and reading better. I couldn't think of a single use for that fancy math, but that made me want it all the more. There must be a use, or no one would have invented it, right? I wanted to learn enough to know what that use might be, just to see.

I was even more worried about Hank and Yance. If I closed the school, would their pa let them keep coming to town? They were studying carpentry with Ike Holstead now, and showing signs of becoming useful, if not yet fit to be let loose on the world. If they had to stop, it might set them back so far they'd settle for the farm. There's nothing wrong with farming, except maybe on this hardscrabble mountain. But I wanted to give them a choice, and that meant giving them time to learn something useful.

After thinking about it all one afternoon, I decided to go out and see the Milgraves and talk about it. To my surprise, Mr. Milgrave, the boys' Pa, was both polite and reasonable. He needed the boys to help with farm work in summer, he said, but he could see that learning a trade might lead to a better life.

Farming up on our mountain isn't much of a way to get rich. Most who try it have to farm a bit, prospect a bit, and do a little of everything else to get by. I don't think anyone around Skunk Corners makes—or grows—enough to keep body and soul together, without at least a bit of hunting and fishing. There are too danged many rocks!

We agreed that Hank and Yance would work mornings on the farm and afternoons with Ike Holstead, who was refurbishing the Mercantile, inside and out.

I was walking home in the evening coolness, well satisfied with my mission, when I encountered the one thing that scares me.

No, not a bear nor yet a courting fellow—I can cope with those. This, my nose told me, was much more unnerving.

A skunk.

I froze in my tracks, my eyes swiveling like they were on lantern-poles, trying to spot the critter without making any move that might startle it.

The little black-and-white animal stepped onto the trail right in front of me, and I turned to stone. I put all my efforts into offering neither threat nor surprise to the thing. I scarce breathed while the critter looked me over and began to saunter up the trail away from me. It was while I considered my options—following a skunk didn't have much appeal, but I needed to get home—that I realized I hadn't seen our town's namesake for a long time.

Maybe not since the Ninja Librarian had so expertly ejected one from the library, his first morning in town.

Now, I like animals, and teach my students respect for all the critters, but I can't say I'd been pining after the skunks. And I was none too happy now to realize I'd have to follow one up the trail, or else take to the woods and beat through the brush in the near-dark.

I decided maybe I'd just set a while on a handy tree trunk and think, while Mr. Skunk, or Mrs. Skunk—I didn't know and didn't care to get close enough to ask—went wherever he, or she, was going.

Thinking about the skunk made me remember that first day, when Tom had thwarted all the plans to drive him off, from ipecac casseroles to toughs bent on fisticuffs—and the skunk, of course. It had been a beautiful sight, a whirl of movement that sent two toughs flying and a skunk into the middle of the eagerly watching townsfolk.

Funny thing, but all those folks who'd been so set against the library were Tom's friends now. Tommy had been ringleader of the skunk gang, and Jake and Harry, who'd thought to beat up the sissy librarian, had ended by asking him to help them learn to read.

I couldn't even remember which of the town's womenfolk had brought those casseroles, but since Tom had brought up a bunch of thrilling stories and subscribed to Godey's Ladies Book for the library, they'd long since dropped their grudge.

I wondered if the skunk could forgive and forget as easily, then laughed at the notion.

The next afternoon, I caught a whiff of skunk out behind the school, and my curious notion of a vengeful skunk returned, despite my refusal to believe in anything so silly.

For the next week, it seemed like every time I went out I smelled skunk.

"It's mating season," Johnny said when I mentioned it. "They get that way."

I didn't tell the barkeep what I was really thinking, but said, "I ain't never smelled them so much any other summer. And around town, too."

Johnny knew as well as I did that we were well past mating time. They'd be raising their families by now.

Tess, too, was dismissive. "This is Skunk Corners. Built around Skunk Springs. There've always been skunks around." Had she forgotten we hadn't seen one in town for over a year? Not since that day at the library.

When I talked to Tom, he made the same sort of noises Tess and Johnny had. But I noticed he kept a sharp eye out when he left the building, and later that day I saw Hank and Yance at work making sure nothing—like a skunk—could get under the front steps.

"Mating season my hindquarters," I muttered as I watched them work.

I said it again when I had to dodge so's not to startle a skunk near the front of the library a day later.

I knew. The critter was holding a grudge.

Tom insisted it was rubbish. "An animal such as a skunk does not possess the intellect to harbor resentment for a year."

Maybe not. But I wasn't going to wander about with Tom, especially not at dusk.

It wasn't Tom who first fell victim, however. It was Tommy. That seemed only fair, since Tommy had trapped the skunk Tom had been forced to eject from the library his first day in town. So really he was the one who had been responsible for the skunk's humiliation that day.

I heard about it from Peggy. She came looking for me in my room, halfway between disgust and laughter.

"Teacher, Tommy needs an awful lot of tomato juice, and a change of clothes."

"What? Oh!"

She didn't wait for me to ask. "Mr. Tom asked

him to trap that skunk that keeps hanging around the library. Tommy figured he could do it, since he—" She broke off and looked guilty.

"Oh, go on. I know all about last time." It'd been all boys in the library that day, but of course she'd known. Probably she'd thought it up, but had sense enough to stay clear. I'd never smelled a hint of skunk about her.

"Well, he was setting the trap, and the skunk walked right up and sprayed him, just like that!"

That was plumb strange.

I was also glad that school was out, because all the tomato juice in the world wouldn't completely remove that smell, and I wouldn't want to be stuck in a stuffy room with it.

I gave Peg an old shirt and a pair of overalls I'd torn up working on the Tavern. They were far too big for Tommy, but they'd get him home. I gave her my last two dollars for tomato juice.

Then I went to see Tom.

He knew, of course. The incident had taken place near the privy out behind the library, and despite closed doors and windows, you could tell.

"Do you believe me yet? I tell you, that's an angry skunk." Or skunks. I didn't like the idea I was having. Had the critter brought friends?

"That does seem unlikely, Alice," Tom said. But I could see the "and yet" in his eyes.

He knew.

Tommy's skunk-trapping efforts didn't help. If anything, we saw the skunk even more. Some around town began muttering about it being a "hydrophoby skunk" and saying someone ought to shoot it before it bit someone.

Neither Tom nor I wanted that. Seemed to me that skunk had been treated plenty bad and had a right to be angry. Tom just didn't like—well, I wasn't sure if he didn't like killing things or if he didn't like guns. Maybe both.

Maybe Tom even felt bad about kicking the thing. But he seemed to figure if he could just sort of remind that skunk who was the Ninja, then it would be over.

I had a hunch it would take something more. Something Tom really wouldn't like.

That was pretty much the way it happened.

Almost.

Tom had gently booted the skunk from the library steps twice, and if he was starting to think he could get away with it, I noticed the critter kept coming back for more.

Like maybe it didn't care who was the Ninja.

I'm pretty sure it was just chance that the final showdown didn't happen at the library, but in the Town Square. What's more, Tom wasn't alone, which is why things got a little out of hand.

Tom had just finished his dinner over at Tess's— like me, he likes Annie's cooking better than his own. He never used to go there much, but quite a few things about Tom seem different these days. Anyway, he started back to the library, and came up with Mayor Burton and his wife, out for an evening stroll.

I hadn't left Tess's yet, so I didn't hear what they said, but I saw Tom stop to speak with them. There was still enough light to see that sour-milk look on Mrs. Burton's face, so I figured she had some gripe or other, probably about the "dreadful, sinful novels" Tom had at the library. She was always afraid folks would read something that would "give them ideas." *She* read nothing but the Holy Book, she claimed. Me, I wondered if she was another one who couldn't read at all.

Seemed to me that ideas were what libraries—and

schools—were about.

Anyway, I watched from the doorway, and was just deciding I'd go have a piece of pie rather than meet up with that pair, when I saw it. A black and white animal humped its way across the Square like a critter with a purpose. And I reckoned I knew what that purpose was.

So I whistled and pointed, and Tom turned just in time to see the tail go up and things begin to happen. There was no way he could stop it now. He was going to get his.

Then he moved. I could hardly even see it, but suddenly he was on the ground, at the end of a long, rolling dive that brought him up twenty feet away and out of the line of fire.

Unfortunately, that left the mayor and his wife right in the skunk's path. And, while the critter might have wished to make a change, it was too late.

They'd have to burn those clothes, if I was any judge.

Tom came to his feet just as the skunk finished and looked around, and he leapt forward before it could move. I thought this time he'd stomp the beast, and the heck with scruples about killing animals. But he hooked it under the belly with his toe and booted it out of the way one more time. It flew, probably cussing a blue streak in whatever passes for lingo among skunks, to land in the brush between the bank and Two Timin' Tess's.

The skunk looked at Tom one last time and saw him looking back. It hesitated just a moment before scuttling off into the dusk at the rate of nobody's business. When I looked back to the Square, the Burtons had scuttled off into the dusk as well, trailing clouds of something that wasn't glory.

I didn't think any of the three would be giving Tom much trouble anytime soon. But I didn't think any of the three would forget anytime soon, either.

9 THE NINJA LIBRARIAN AND THE BOYS FROM ENDOLINE

When word about the skunk incident got around, people started looking at the Ninja Librarian with a whole new kind of respect. I mean, they'd known he was smart, though many didn't much care about that. And they'd known he was tough—tough enough to handle our worst library-hating specimens, and smart enough to have taught them to read. But none of us had realized he was so fast.

I'd seen the whole thing, unlike most folks, and I was impressed. That dive he used to get out of range in the instant between the lifting of the skunk's talk and the arrival of the spray had been so fast and so smooth that I still couldn't believe it. It was beautiful and I wanted to be able to do that.

It led me to do a foolish thing.

I asked Tom where he'd learned to be a Ninja.

"I have told you that I practice daily, as I hope you do."

Well, that was no kind of answer to the question I'd asked. I pushed it. "But, well, is there some kind of Ninja Librarian school or something?"

"I believe that 'or something' would be the more accurate answer, though deplorable English."

Then he made me practice for an extra hour, so by the time I got to Tess's the stew was all gone and I had to settle for a slab of yesterday's cornbread.

Sometimes I think he does that on purpose.

It was only a couple of days later that I started noticing them. Not skunks this time. Young men, boys really, coming into town from—somewhere. They weren't exactly intimidating. For one thing, most of them weren't much older than Tommy. But any collection of strangers in Skunk Corners would've made me uneasy, and it was worse because I couldn't figure out why they were here. All I knew was that they had to be up to something. Boys always were.

School being out, it took a bit to track down my own young fry. My students, I mean. When I found Tommy—not down by the creek where I expected him, but over at the depot—he shrugged.

"They ain't talked to me, Teacher." I could tell by his grin that he knew darn well he should've said "haven't," so I sort of didn't hear the "ain't." You learn, after a while.

"But you don't have any idea?" I pressed.

"Nope. They just come around, mostly nose about the school and the library, and head out by chore time."

I knew all that. Were they looking to disrupt our library? They'd be in for a surprise if they tried. Or if they messed with the school.

For want of a better idea, I asked Tommy, "Speaking of chore time, what about you? Are you getting home to help your Ma at all?"

He gave me that grin again. "Ma says if'n I milk the cow mornin' and night, and keep the woodbox full, I can slope off when the kids are awake." Tommy's got two sets of twin brothers, two and three years old. I hoped they'd tame down a lot before they started school. His Ma was awfully generous to let Tommy off so easy. Likely I wasn't hearing the whole story, and soon or late it'd catch up to him.

By the end of a week, I had a few more ideas about the strangers. At any rate, I knew the boys—some, anyway—were from up around Endoline.

I'd recognized one of them. Ryan was old enough I'd been in school with him up there for a year or so. He'd changed some from the little kid I'd known, but I couldn't mistake that shock of coal-black hair. Nor the scar on his forehead.

"I was there the day he picked that up," I explained to Tom. "He got into a scrap after school with a kid twice his age. Twice his size, too." He'd been little then, but now Ryan must be pushing fifteen, and he was pretty much full-grown.

"I hadn't realized there was a school in Endoline," Tom commented.

"Oh, now and again. Mostly not. Those times, my Pa taught me. He wasn't precisely an educated man, not like you. But he dearly loved books, and he knew enough to get me started." It was getting easier to speak of Pa, after all this time. But I still had to look away and swallow hard.

"And you just kind of kept going."

I shrugged.

"You know that makes you a bit unusual," he pressed.

I shrugged again. Seemed to me there wasn't much about me that was "usual," and it didn't do me much good. Look at how I dress, and I can't act like a girl come heck or high water. I don't even want to, which is really different from the other girls.

I've just got to be *doing* stuff, and girls are meant to sit still, seems like.

None of that got us any closer to knowing what those boys from Endoline were doing hanging around Skunk Corners.

"If they're thinking to cause trouble for my students, they'll wish they hadn't." The same was true if they had evil intentions toward the library, but no need for me to say that. Tom could see to the library, and I needn't worry.

"I don't know," Tom said slowly, like maybe he was thinking it out as he went. "Seems like if they were looking for trouble they'd have found it by now."

That was true. Even if Hank and Yance were too busy with Ike Holstead and the Mercantile to get into fights, Tommy wasn't, nor Joey or Lije. Joey was only ten, but Lije—Eljah Monroe—had said he was twelve when he started coming to school last winter. If so, he was big for his age. He'd fight, alright, if the opportunity presented itself.

Some of the girls weren't so slow either, though Peg, who was oldest and biggest, was too smart for fisticuffs. She'd clobber them without getting her hands dirty. But she reported no trouble.

Along about then, I got distracted, and stopped fretting about those boys. Seeing as they weren't causing any trouble, I decided I had bigger fish to fry.

I wanted to know what'd become of Billy Jenkins' Pa.

Even though Billy was pretty happy living with Tess and her crew, I kind of kept an eye on him. So when he got kind of glum, I had to know why.

"Aw, Teacher, it's almost my birthday."

"I know," I said, not quite truthfully. "You're going to be seven."

"Yup. And always on my birthday," he gulped and went on, "my Pa takes me off for a day on the mountain."

"Well, I guess I could do that," I offered.

He looked away, and I knew I wasn't what he wanted. "Thanks, Teacher. But," he studied the floor by his toes with great interest, not wanting to look at me. "But you ain't my Pa."

Now it was my turn to stare at the floor. We were in Johnny's barroom, and it was plenty scuffed up. I didn't find any answers there, only the scratches and stains of years of hard use, plus the deep gouges the tree had left.

"Well," I said at last. "No, I reckon I'm not. And maybe I can't give you just what your Pa does. But I'll do something real special for you."

"What?" He demanded, suspicious.

I had no idea what. I was making this up as I went along. Seemed like that was the story of my life. I bought myself some time. "It'll be a surprise."

I didn't know what I'd do for Billy's birthday, but I knew one thing. I'd find his Pa if he was on the sunny side of the sod, and I'd bring him back no matter how long it took.

I set in to figure it out the next day. The trouble was, the first thing I needed was to find out what Ina Jenkins knew, and I didn't figure she'd talk to me. Probably just haul off and shoot me if I came near her.

Nor would she talk to Tess, or to Tom.

So who could I send to find out if she knew where her husband had gone? I thought about Preacher Dawson, but didn't figure she'd be any nicer to him just because he's a man of the cloth. She didn't seem like the religious sort.

Jake. I needed Crazy Jake, Billy's uncle, and brother to the missing man. If he didn't know where Bill Jenkins was, he might be the only person Ina would talk to.

I sighed. To talk to Jake, I'd have to jump the midnight train up to Endoline, and probably hike back down. It's not such a long hike—those boys were doing it nearly every day, and for no good reason I could see. It's just that I'd not been back since I walked out of town, two years after my Pa died and two hours after it became clear I couldn't live there alone any longer.

I had never told anyone about that day, because I didn't even want to remember it. Going anywhere near Endoline would force me to. I resented that, even more than being forced to hike down from Endoline in the middle of the night.

Nevertheless, midnight found me waiting by the depot, and I swung up into the caboose just as the train started to move. I wasn't giving Jake any chance to blow the whistle and throw me off.

Jake had climbed up just before me, having inspected all the couplings and emptied the slop buckets. There wasn't much glamor in his job, but he was pleased to have it.

He jumped when I came in off the back platform, once we were moving well.

"Al! What in tarnation are you doing here?"

"I need to talk to you."

His eyes narrowed with suspicion, and I hurried to add, "about your brother. About Billy's Pa."

"What about Bill?"

"Do you know where he is?" No point in beating around the bush.

Jake shook his head. "I ain't heard from him all spring."

"Do you know where he set off to? See here, Jake,

Billy needs his Pa. He'd probably settle for you, but it's his Pa he wants."

Jake looked sad. "I feel bad," he muttered, "running out on the sprout that way,"

"Forget it," I told him without sympathy. "You need this job, and you want to keep a safe distance from that she-viper your brother married."

"Never did see why he did that," Jake grumbled.

"Me neither, but never mind that. Where did Bill take off to?"

"All I know is he said he was goin' prospecting. Then he didn't come back."

"And you never worried?" I wondered if Jake might be stupid after all. This went beyond the lack of common sense that guided most everything he did. "You didn't go looking? Tarnation, Jake, he could've been hurt." Or killed, I didn't need to add. "And you just left it?"

"Naw, Al, it wasn't like that!" Jake seemed eager not to have me think so poorly of him. "I got a letter, asked me to let him be a while. He'd be back when he'd took care of some business. Fact is," he looked away, abashed. "Fact is, I figured he just couldn't stand Ina no more."

"Why'd he go and leave his boy?" I couldn't muster the sympathy Bill's plight deserved.

But Jake had no more answers, and I had a long walk home. I left the train when it slowed outside Endoline. I wasn't going back to that place.

By concentrating on Bill Jenkins, I managed to keep my mind from traveling to the empty cabin just out the other side of town.

On my way down the mountain, I met the boys who'd been haunting Skunk Corners, on their way up. They were late on the trail this time, and too many for comfort, so I just faded into the woods and let them pass.

There he was again, the kid I'd known. Ryan.
Again I wondered what they were up to. It beat
wondering how I was going to find Bill Jenkins, who
maybe didn't want to be found.

Two days later, though I still had no idea how to
find Billy's Pa—or what to do for his birthday—I
learned what Ryan and his pals wanted. It shocked
me to the soles of my boots.

They caught me one night headed into the library.
A couple grabbed each my arms and insisted on
coming in with me. I could have fought, but it was
easy to see they meant no harm, so I let them march
me up the stairs. Though if they'd tried to take me
anywhere but the library, where I knew Tom was
waiting for me, I'd have kicked alright, and those
boys would've known I objected.

Once inside, I twitched their hands loose.

"No need to grab, boys. Waddaya want?"

I could see Tom in the shadows, though Ryan and
his friends didn't seem to. I noticed the other boys
were all younger, only twelve or thirteen, I'd guess.
There were five of them, and they all had a look I
recognized. The look of young things that needed
help. I had a sudden realization and my questions
evaporated. No. Oh, no.

"We want a school," Ryan said.

I'd have run then, but the Ninja Librarian was
blocking the door.

It took an hour, and a lot of help from Tom, but
eventually we had a deal. They got two hours a day,
and they'd pay me in meat, potatoes, pennies,
whatever they could scrounge. I'd teach them to
read, write, and do basic arithmetic, and Tom would
let them use the library—even give them library
cards.

"And if any books are ruined or stolen," he pointed out, "you will regret it with all your being."

And then, as they were leaving, I had my idea. I knew what I would do for Billy's birthday.

10 THE NINJA LIBRARIAN GETS IT WRONG

So I had some work that summer to keep me out of trouble. I started right in. I told those boys to be at the schoolhouse an hour after daybreak—just long enough to get there from Endoline if they left at first light. That way we'd be done before it got too hot. Otherwise, we'd have to hold our summer school in the creek.

Of course, if I had any problems with any of them roughs, I'd throw him in the creek, which might be a lesson in itself.

They were there, all six of them, when I came out next morning, with a motley assortment of money and goods to pay me. They filed into the school, looking as solemn as though this were a matter of life and death.

Come to think of it, if learning to read was their ticket out of Endoline, it might well be life and death.

That first day I didn't try to do much besides learn their names and see what they knew.

"Teacher," said one—he said his name was Benny—"we ain't had a teacher up at Endoline in years. We don't know *nuthin'*. Not letters, not words, not nuthin'."

I glanced at Ryan who, I knew, had at least been to school a bit, but he looked away, so I didn't ask, not just then. And when I started testing, he matched his answers to the other boys', so it looked as though none of them knew so much as A, B, C.

But I kept Ryan after school a minute, until the others had gone out.

"What're you playing at, Ryan? I remember you, and I know you went to school some. Long enough to get that scar, anyhow." I pointed, and he responded with a sheepish grin.

"I'd hoped you'd forgot." He hesitated, then said, "Look, the others don' know. That I been to school, I mean. Especially that I know how to read. A little, anyway," he finished.

I just looked my question.

"They wouldn't have come if'n I didn't, so I had to make like I'd never been."

"Okay. I reckon I can see your point." That was only half true. I couldn't see why him wanting to learn more would scare them off, but he knew them best. "I'll give some thought to how we can make this worth your while without giving you away."

"Somethin' else, Teacher."

His tone made me look.

"They don't know yer from Endoline. And I ain't gonna tell 'less you do."

"No," I said, thinking. "Let's just keep that between us two."

I sat for a while after Ryan left, trying not to

think.

It was definitely best if my students didn't know I was from their home town.

I came out of the school just before noon, when it had gotten too hot in there to study any more. I had reached Chapter Four in that Advanced Algebra book, and had spent three hours trying to understand what it meant.

I turned toward the library without even thinking about it. I needed something else to read. Stories, if Tom would give me any. Maybe history. That's stories, too, but on account of they're true, they aren't allowed to write them up as interesting as the made-up kind.

Tom wasn't in the library, though it was open. Peggy sat behind the desk, looking very important, though there was no one else in the place just then.

"Hi, Teacher. Mr. Tom said I could be the librarian while he helps the boys with some stuff."

I was surprised, since Peggy was very careful not to be left out of things.

She guessed what I was thinking. "Oh, I helped with the design. This is just the part where they move stuff around. It's hot out there." She didn't need to say more. While she sat in the cool, shaded library, all the boys—and the Ninja Librarian—were out in the sun, getting hot and dirty.

Nope, there's nothing wrong with Peggy Rossiter's brains.

"So what's the plan this time?" I asked. I was less worried than I would've been a while back. None of the recent experiments had blown up.

"We're gonna run a pipe over from the spring, but we'll put it right atop that mess of dark rocks."

The teacher in me said, "The basalt outcrop, you mean."

"Right, Teacher. Tommy and me noticed they

get real hot, these sunny days, so we thought maybe they could warm the water, a little, anyhow."

I felt a surge of excitement. This one might really work.

Though a nagging part of my brain wondered. Seemed like there was a flaw, somewhere.

Soon I was wallowing happily in a pile of books. Tom had left three for me—two histories and a book on Latin. I had my own thoughts about that. What I was reading, though, was Miss Alcott's *Little Men* and an interesting true story about ships called *Two Years Before the Mast*. I swapped back and forth every few pages, because I couldn't make up my mind between adventure and a sort of mysteriously lovely vision of a home like nothing and nowhere I'd ever seen.

I forgot all about lunch.

Eventually Tom came back, looking very slightly smudged, but satisfied.

"Did you get all the pipe laid?" I asked innocently, as Peg darted off to find the boys, no doubt meaning to join them in the creek.

"Ah. I did assume Peggy would explain to you. We have positioned much of the pipeline, but my assistants will need to acquire more pipe to finish the job."

I stood there and glared, my hands on my hips. "Are you letting those boys *steal* for your bath?"

"Alice, I would have thought you knew me better than that," he reproved me. "They have taken it from a long-abandoned mine." He didn't let me say any more. "Time for your lesson, is it not?"

He might've worked me to the dropping point, but I didn't forget my worries. If those boys weren't stealing the pipe, they were risking their necks around an old mine to get it. Being from elsewhere, Tom might not understand about old mines, but I did.

Of course, by the time Tom had finished with me, the youngsters had all gone off home, looking for dinner. I did the same, grumbling to myself the while.

Next day was Billy Jenkins' birthday, and I pushed aside my worries to carry out my plan. Collecting him from the Tavern just before sunrise, I brought him to the school in time to ring the bell and let in Ryan and the boys from Endoline. I perched Billy on my stool in front of the class. The boys looked from him to me, bewildered.

"Billy here is going to teach you your ABCs," I explained. "He'll show you it's so easy a child of six can do it."

"I'm seven," Billy said.

"Yes, but you learned to read when you were six."

He nodded. "That's true," he said seriously. "And now that I'm older, I can teach it. I remember how."

I hid a smile and watched my summer students. I hoped they would go along with this, and to my relief, they did. Maybe they were too confused to argue. Maybe they were being nice to a little kid. And maybe they just figured this was normal.

Billy began solemnly—and accurately—to reproduce my first lesson in letters. I relaxed as he moved into the spirit of the thing, calling on students in turn to come write the letters on my big slate.

I decided I had, as well as I could, given him what his Pa did on birthdays: I'd made him important and given him a place in the adult world for the day.

Then I sighed. It's too bad that the adult world only looks like a place you want to be when you're too young to stay there long. It looked like I was good and stuck there, and it wasn't so much fun.

At the end of the two-hour lesson, those boys could write half the letters and could sing the alphabet song all through. They'd kicked a bit about that, and I'd had to step in and explain that singing things makes us remember them better than anything else, and if they learned that song, they'd know all the letters without even breaking a sweat.

When they'd gone, Billy sat down at my desk with a big grin.

"I think I learned them pretty good." He leaned back and put his hands behind his head, the way Johnny does when relaxing after dinner.

"I think you *taught* them very *well*," I said like any school marm. "You seem to have a knack for it."

"Mebbe I'll be a teacher when I grow up," he said. "If I don't decide to be a bartender."

That was one worry off my mind; two if you count the teaching. But I had more. I returned Billy to Tess, and went to the library.

Tom was there, alone but for Mrs. Herberts, who was looking for something to read when it was too hot to work. Which, in my opinion, was pretty much all the time just now.

I waited until she was gone, then faced Tom. "So. Where have those kids been getting the pipe?"

"They didn't say, exactly, Alice. As long as the mine was truly abandoned, and they assured me it is, I saw no reason for concern."

"That is just where you are wrong." I surprised both of us with the vehemence of my declaration.

"Old mines are dangerous, and if they aren't stealing, they're still taking an awful chance."

I could see he hadn't realized this. Tom's pretty good at hiding his feelings, but I'm learning to read them anyway.

"I see."

I waited.

"I believe they have gone over the ridge above the spring. I imagine you could track them. The pipe has made a bit of a path, as they were forced to drag it."

I was mad enough that I didn't wait to see if he'd follow. I just stormed out of there, but when I emerged from my rooms a minute later, with a rope and a flask of water, Tom waited for me. The library was closed.

"Aren't Hank and Yance supposed to be working for Ike Holstead, when they aren't on the farm?" It was almost a change of subject.

"Their father informs me it is too hot for farm work after breakfast. And Mr. Holstead is only working in the evenings just now. So I thought I should put the young men to work."

I couldn't fault that logic, though I did wonder about them tramping over the mountains in this heat. There was a reason folks weren't working just now. And I really didn't like what the kids were doing and where they had gone. I charged up the ridge at top speed, despite the heat.

We picked up the youngsters' trail easily, as Tom had expected. At least, we could see where they'd been before, and it was a safe bet they'd gone back to the same place for more pipe.

I don't know why I was so convinced they'd get into trouble this time, when they'd been to the mine before without incident. I guess I just figured their luck had to run out sometime. Tom had caught my worry, too, and once over the ridge we nearly ran down the trail they'd left.

In fact, we didn't slow until we spotted a flock of young folks coming toward us, dragging long sections of rusty pipes travois-fashion.

Suddenly, I felt abashed. I'd gone charging off on a rescue mission for a bunch of mountain-bred youngsters who didn't need rescuing. Never mind that my experience with Jake and Harry had taught me that growing up in Skunk Corners didn't prove a fellow knew his right foot from his left, let alone how to wander the hills without dying. These were my kids, the ones I knew had more sense than that pair, as if anyone could have less.

I came very near to giving myself away by turning to flee, but Tom demonstrated that his lightning-fast Ninja reflexes weren't just physical.

"Ah, there you are. Your teacher and I thought we ought to come and lend a hand, as we will be the primary beneficiaries of the hot water." As though it was an afterthought, he added, "Old mines are dangerous, and I ought not to have encouraged you to explore such an area. But, of course, you are aware of that and I have utter confidence in your good sense and caution."

"Oh, yeah, of course, Mr. Tom," they chorused.

"Thanks for coming to help out," Peggy added, handing over her pipes to me and wiping her brow.

All the way back to town I struggled between admiration for Tom's quick thinking and annoyance that he'd saddled me with a hard job on a hot day. He'd explained the rope I carried by saying we'd "thought it might be more expeditious to rope several lengths of pipe together for transport."

Well, it was and it wasn't, but it did give us an excuse to sit in the shade and watch all the boys and Peggy struggle to truss up the awkward bundle. When they finished, we all laid hold on the ropes and hauled the lot on up and over the hill.

When we finally reached the school, we dropped our burden and headed in a body for the creek, leaving Tom where he stood. Didn't the man ever sweat?

Once we'd all landed in the swimming hole—fully clothed since our stuff needed washing anyway—I admonished the children.

"You know mines are dangerous. I don't want any of you going back there!"

"Aw, Teacher, we didn't go near the holes," Tommy protested.

"Anyway," Peggy added, "We have what we need now and I, for one, am not climbing that hill again. Not until it's about a hundred degrees cooler."

"'Right. But stay away from those places. You never know," I began. My speech about safety and good sense was doomed to remain unsaid. We heard a bloodcurdling yell and saw a blur of white hair and black mask.

The Ninja Librarian landed with a giant splash in the middle of the swimming hole. When he surfaced, we all stared. He wore a white and black striped garment that looked an awful lot like a union suit, and his Ninja mask. With great dignity, he said, "I believe this is the fashion in men's swimwear now in some parts of the country."

I guess maybe even a Ninja Librarian gets it wrong now and again.

11 THE NINJA LIBRARIAN GETS INTO HOT WATER

After a week of my impromptu summer school with Billy now my regular assistant, Ryan and his cronies were assembling letters into words. Rather, the other boys were. Ryan, since he already knew how to read, at least sort of, was working on the Third Reader. The covers were all pretty much alike, so none of the others noticed.

They'd all been working away for the better part of an hour that morning, reading and writing their words and trying to make sense of it all, when I rapped for attention.

"Okay, class. You've got a good start on reading. What do you know of arithmetic?"

To my surprise, most of them knew more about numbers than letters, though on reflection I should have known. They figured money, and played dice and card games, so they had to learn a bit of addition and subtraction, or get taken for everything they had.

Besides, Buddy said, "Numbers are *real*, Teacher. You gotta know how many of whatever you have, and putting two with two has to make four. You can see it. Letters and words, them things are just made up, so they're harder to learn."

We laughed, but it made me think. I took the comment to the Ninja Librarian later.

"In a way, Alice, the young man is correct. Though he may not think numbers so natural when he reaches the higher mathematics. Yet even that is based on real things."

"I'll bet," I muttered. Advanced Algebra was still giving me grief, though I had managed to grasp Chapter Four well enough to move on. I was afraid to ask Peggy where she was with it.

"Once letters have been given meaning," Tom continued, "they too become real. Their sound is their sound, at least as long as you stick to English."

"Except when it's not," I pointed out. I was still thinking about Algebra. I needed a teacher, and it would have made sense to ask Tom for help. I just didn't want to, maybe for fear he'd think me stupid, and maybe for fear I'd find out he didn't know the stuff, either.

In any case, I had bigger fish to fry. So did he. Tom was busy early and late assembling the water pipes over the basalt, the stretch of dark volcanic rock that got so hot in summer that he believed it could heat water.

Me, I'd gotten an idea. The children's expedition to that nearby mine made me wonder about Billy's Pa. Way I saw it, unless he was dead, he'd either gone off so far he'd never make it back—or he'd gone "prospecting" around the old mines holed up somewhere to do the thinking he'd mentioned to Jake. He'd been gone since early in the winter, so if he'd not been prepared, odds were he was dead. But I kind of thought he'd gone off a-purpose. Maybe he didn't want to be found, but I didn't care. Billy needed a father, if Bill Jenkins could be persuaded to be one.

The youngsters had said there was no sign anyone else had been around their mine anytime lately. But I knew of at least a half-dozen other mines that had been started and abandoned within a day's walk of Skunk Corners.

Of course, there was no reason for Bill Jenkins to have stayed close. I just sort of figured a man might stick to an area he knew, especially if he was out there for something other than gold. Though what he was doing for supplies I didn't know. Maybe going down to Lupine or Pine Knot.

So I took to roaming the hills in the afternoons and evenings, wandering farther and farther in search of any sign that someone was out there.

And all the while I was doing that, Tom and his crew were laying pipe, and adjusting the windmill on the ridge to pump with enough force to push the water through about a half mile of extra pipes.

He also, in keeping with their new training as carpenters, or at least builders, had Hank and Yance building a bathhouse in the woods back of the school.

Since that put it closer to my digs than to Tom's quarters in the library, I'd have thought it a generous gesture, had not running the water directly into the library from the springs meant crossing the road. It was just more practical to keep it on my side. Not that I was complaining.

So the summer slipped along towards July. It got hotter, and I still found no signs of anyone living away back in the hills.

That didn't stop me looking. To be honest, I kind of liked the search, for the chance to wander the hills. Maybe that was why I was so sure Bill Jenkins had just gone off to be alone—because I enjoyed doing the same thing.

If I didn't find Billy's missing father, I did find peace, quiet, and five new swimming holes, including one with a waterfall that made a perfect place to wash my short-cropped hair. Though it took a truly hot afternoon to make the icy cascade appealing, hot afternoons we had in plenty.

I'd thought the previous summer was hot, but this one was shaping up to be even worse, if something didn't happen to break the heat.

I hadn't realized that Ryan and the other boys from Endoline were no longer going right home after lessons. They'd begun going to the library to get the books Tom had promised—one each, and trade them in whenever they finished—now that they could begin to puzzle out what they said. This allowed Tom to pass Ryan more challenging reading, while trying to figure out where his talents lay. Besides in fighting, of course. *That* skill would only keep him in Endoline, or worse.

I'd come in early from my expedition to the hills, too hot to carry on, and found the whole lot—plus most of my regular students—heads down in their books. It gave me a start to see that Peggy was on Chapter Six of "Advanced Algebra," because I'd only just finished Chapter Four. We were definitely going to need a different approach to teaching that subject.

Peggy looked up when I came in.

"Teacher, do you know what MaryBeth said?"

"I have no idea."

"She says her Pa says girls don't need to learn math beyond simple fractions, because that's all you need to cook."

A couple of the boys giggled, and she silenced them with a glare that could have frozen water even on this dog-day.

"Cooking's important," Ryan suggested.

"Yes, it is," Peggy countered. "I suggest you learn, if you want to eat all your life." She turned back to me while the children giggled again, this time at Ryan's stunned expression. "Then MaryBeth said that her Pa said girls can't learn higher math anyway, because our brains aren't made for it."

"Well, you know that's not true."

"That's just *it*. Since you and I—and Janey, too—are all doing it, seems to me Mr. Burton doesn't know what he's talking about."

"A reasonable conclusion," put in Tom. I waited to see where Peggy was going with this.

"So," she went on, frustration and bewilderment pushing her lower lip out, "how did a guy that knows so little get to be *mayor*?"

Well, I just looked at her. Then I looked at the rest of the gang, and we all looked at Tom, who looked back.

"I have no idea," I said at last, and every head nodded in agreement.

"I would presume there was an election," Tom suggested.

"But when? I don't recall any such thing." I turned to Hank and Yance. "You two should remember back to before I came. Do you recall any election?"

The twins shook their heads. We all looked at Peg again.

"So maybe he's no mayor at all," she concluded for us. "Certainly he is a very ignorant man, if he doesn't know women are just as good as men."

I saw the boys from Endoline shift a little, as though they wanted to argue the point. Then they looked from Peg to me and back, and decided to keep quiet. I always knew they were smart boys.

I wasn't sure I liked where Peg was going with this. I wasn't ready for another fight just now, so I changed the subject, some.

"I was wondering, Ryan. Are there no school-aged girls in Endoline?"

He looked from me to Peg and swallowed hard. "Yes, Ma'am. There surely are."

"And?"

"This is too far for a girl to walk, Teacher."

Peg snorted. I tried lifting an eyebrow, the way the Ninja Librarian does when he's dubious about something you've said. He was doing it now.

"Well, um," Ryan tried.

A scrawny kid with unruly blond hair tried to explain. "Most folk up home think like your mayor. Girls don't need learnin' 'cause they're just getting' married. Learnin' would give 'em ideas."

"*Ideas* are the general intention," I pointed out. He turned red.

"Er."

"Any of you boys have sisters? Or know any girls who haven't yet been turned into mindless slaves?"

They looked at each other, not sure how to respond. Finally, Melville ventured, "I guess my sister might like to come. She's eleven, so I reckon she could manage to hike down here."

"But we ain't got no more money, nor nothin' else, to pay for them," Benny pointed out.

"Fine," I said. "I don't care. Just get them here."

By this time, I'd forgotten what I'd come for, so I got a book and went back to my room, where I read until it was too dark to see, then went and took my lesson in Ninja fighting down in the library basement. Along about midnight, I showed up at Tess's hoping for a meal of some sort. Two-Timin' Tess's being a tavern, it was still open, though the few remaining patrons had little interest in food.

Tess herself brought me some stew and a slab of pie.

"Saved it for you. I saw you going to the library for your lesson and knew you'd be hungry."

"Thanks," I mushed out around a mouthful of the pie. It was above-average good, which was only to be expected. Annie didn't make food that wasn't worth going out of your way for.

I was glad that the Endoline crew had scraped together enough cash to pay me, so I could keep eating at Tess's. They'd brought two chickens as well, and I'd turned those over to Tess in exchange for several days' eating.

Tess broke into my thoughts of food. "I hear you've been looking for Billy's Pa."

"Yup."

"Seen any sign yet?"

"Nope."

Tess toyed with her tea cup. "I'm wondering if it's a good idea."

That got my full attention at last. "What? Why ever not?"

"I'm thinking of Billy. Getting his hopes up. But what if you don't find him? Or you do, and he won't come?" Or he was dead, we were both thinking.

It made sense, to a point. Billy was young, and he was settling in nicely at Tess's. Maybe it would be better to let sleeping dogs lie. Did I even know if Bill Jenkins would be good for the boy if I did find him? After all, he'd left him once.

For all that, it struck me something was out of whack with Tess's argument. There was something she wasn't telling me. I snuck a look at her. Tess was as good as Tom at wearing an unreadable face. Not for the first time I thought they must've sprung from the same unlikely source. If she didn't want to tell me, there was no use my prying.

Not to her face, anyway.

But if there was a reason Tess Noreen didn't want me prying around the old mines, you could bet I was going to find it out.

Later, I wondered if that was what Tess had wanted. She knows me so well.

Next morning at sunup there were four girls with the six boys outside the school. Three were about ten or eleven years old, but the fourth was pushing sixteen, if I wasn't mistaken.

"My name's Francine," she offered before I could ask. "I heard tell you was teaching folks to read down here, and I wanna learn."

I looked around, wondering whose sister she was. Ryan shook his head. "Franny don't belong to any of us, Teacher. But her Pa's awful set on her marrying ol' Coot Mulligan."

She crossed her arms and set her face. "And I ain't gonna. So I figure I need a little learnin' before I light out for elsewhere."

I nodded, thinking. I'd teach the girl to read and write. But I'd better get Tess or Hilda to teach her the rest of what she'd need to know if she was going out in the world.

I got Billy to help me. He started the girls on their ABCs whilst I taught the boys how to figure out what a new word meant. Billy was a natural for teaching, and the girls all gushed over him, just like girls anywhere. I hoped they'd all had permission to come, and no one would get a lickin' for being out all day.

I spent the hottest part of the afternoon hunting around the back side of the ridge for a mine I'd heard tell of. I got back hot, dirty, and tired, and the whole pipe-laying crew met me in a state of high excitement.

"Teacher! It's all ready! The bath house and everything!" They led me into the woods a little way, and sure enough, a small, rough shed stood in a little clearing near the basalt flow. Pipes led in at the back.

Tom stood there, towel and soap in hand, looking pleased and eager.

"I believe we are ready for our first hot bath," he announced. "Behold!"

Tommy swung open the door and I looked in. A trough-sized tub stood in the middle of the small room, filled with water that steamed energetically even in the late-afternoon heat. The temperature inside the shed must've been nigh a hundred, and I backed out in a hurry.

"It's your project, Mr. Tom. You have the first bath. Me, I'll just nip down to the creek."

The kids and I had sunk blissfully into the cool creek water in the swimming hole, and I started to say, "I really look forward to..." when we all heard a yell. Then silence.

A moment later, the same white-and-black blur we'd seen before came flying down the path and landed in the middle of the swimming hole once again.

Seemed to me he was a bit red around the edges, like a boiled crawdad.

When he surfaced, Tom looked around at all of us watching him. "The water seemed a trifle warm, so I thought I'd join you here instead."

"Well," I consoled him, "Think how good it'll feel on a cold winter day."

Only when I heard Peggy's soft "oh!" did it register on me. Those rocks weren't going to be so warm on cold winter days.

We still had some work to do.

12 BIG AL GETS IT WRONG

I had to wait until Saturday to carry out my plan to hunt up and search some of the more distant mines on our mountain, since I'd found no sign of Bill Jenkins closer in. I'd need to stay away overnight, and I couldn't do that when I had a room full of students eager to absorb whatever knowledge I might toss their way. Not when they worked so hard just to get there.

I'd sent Francine to Tess after school that first day, and I wasn't sure if the girl had gone home at all. From what she'd told me, and knowing all too much about Endoline, it might be as well if she didn't. But how many more strays could Tess afford to take in?

I wouldn't think about that. Right now I needed to find Bill Jenkins—and I wanted to find out why Tess was trying to discourage me poking around the mines. It sure as heck wasn't because she was afraid I'd hurt myself, because she knew me better than that. I also wanted to stay clear of Peggy, who was still troubled by our mayor's qualifications—or lack of them. I didn't know what she expected me to do about it, but I could tell from her gaze that she expected something. So leaving town for a day or two looked like a good idea.

I headed out at the crack of dawn, but not early enough to beat the Ninja Librarian. He was in the bath house, singing "Suwannee River" while he ran water into the tub. He had a nice voice and he knew all the words. It made a welcome change from the singing that sometimes came from Tess's late at night.

He interrupted himself to explain. "I'm filling it halfway with cool water. At the end of the afternoon, I will fill it the rest of the way with the very hot water. That should make for a bath of just about the right temperature."

I grinned at him. "For now, I like my creek water. But we have to find a way to heat water in the winter. That's when I want a hot bath, not on a dog-day like this."

"I am giving it due consideration, Alice. To whence are you traveling?" He'd seen my pack. I'd rolled a loaf of bread, a tin mug, and some dried soup fixings into a blanket, tied the ends shut, and slung it over my shoulder. I didn't figure I'd need much, hot as it was. It hadn't even been cooling down nights.

"I'm off to enjoy a day or two in the hills. Too many folks in town these days."

Tom looked down the dusty street, which at the moment was crowded with a sleeping dog and a raven inspecting to see if it was dead, and nodded. "Yes, I can see how that might be a problem." I didn't figure I was fooling him any.

I'd gone a dozen paces before I turned back. "Do you think I'm doing the right thing, Tom?

Tess wonders if it would be better if I didn't go."

Tom stopped smiling. "I do not know, Alice. We may only know—when you find him."

Huh. The Ninja Librarian seemed to have a lot fewer answers these days. I wondered if that meant he'd gotten dumber—or smarter.

Wasn't a librarian supposed to completely answer all your questions?

I enjoyed my Saturday out. By the hottest part of the afternoon, I was high enough in the mountains that a steady breeze cooled me nicely.

Of course, I'd have to go back down, once I'd checked out the tiny remains of a mine I'd spotted up on Skunk Peak. I didn't expect to find Bill Jenkins there—winters were too hard at that elevation—but I had to look.

I did see signs of digging, but a closer look told me it was marmots, or coyotes chasing ground squirrels. Nothing human, so I headed on down the far side of the ridge, sweating even going downhill, as I dropped out of reach of the breeze.

I took a sighting on the spot down valley where I had the highest hopes, the big scar that marked the site of the Lucky Louse mine. It hadn't proved so lucky for the louse who'd found it. He'd spent five years digging before it collapsed on him, leaving him both dead broke and just plain dead.

At least, that was the story. All the mines around our mountain had been left to rot long before I was born. None had been worth the sweat and blood the prospectors and miners poured into them, though riches enough were pulled out of the ground practically within shouting distance of us. Somehow, our area just never seemed to have any luck. Just like the Louse.

With all that, logic should've said Bill Jenkins would've gone where the mines had been rich, far from our mountain. Thing is, those rich mines had all been dug out, or else they still had folks working them. If he mostly just wanted to get lost, but still maybe find a little gold, our hills would work just fine. And the Lucky Louse had a cabin, of sorts.

I kept a sharp eye out while I walked. Not just for Mr. Jenkins, either. There were a few skunks, and at least one mountain lion, that might be holding some kind of grudge after meeting the Ninja Librarian. They'd maybe retreated up here. I wasn't taking any chances, just in case they remembered me, too. I had my Bowie knife, but that wouldn't help much against a skunk.

I reached the Lucky Louse just before sunset, and I didn't run right up to it. Instead, I hung back in the willows along the creek and watched a bit, not wanting to spook anyone.

I didn't see a thing.

After a half hour, I got hungry, so I gave up being sneaky and headed for the cabin, which was half logs and half cave. I hollered a bit, just to be sure no one would shoot at me, and to make sure the skunks or whatever had fair warning I was coming. If no human lived there, odds were the critters would've moved in. They might not like me coming to visit, and I didn't want trouble.

The cabin might have been unoccupied, but I could see as I drew near that it wasn't untended. Once inside I was sure of it. Everything was in good repair, neat and clean. The stove had been set up and a chimney rigged from scrap, the original having rusted away long since.

I grinned in triumph. If Bill Jenkins wasn't living here now, I'd bet my summer wages—if I'd had any to speak of—that he had been, and would be again. The neatness of things argued against him being dead. He'd have been unlikely to have swept the hearth and taken away his blankets before going out to fall down a mine shaft or be buried in an avalanche. Why I was so sure it was Bill Jenkins, I don't know, but I was. I'd not heard of anyone else up here.

Since it was getting dark, I settled into that cabin and hoped Bill Jenkins would show up in the morning.

Out on the mountain all day, I'd been thinking that I could sure see why someone would want to come off up here and just stay. But I can tell you, when it got to be night and the coyotes began to sing, it felt lonely, up there all alone. I don't hate coyotes, like some folks in Skunk Corners do, but come dusk their song is enough to make a body want to cry.

Come Sunday morning, I made myself some pine-bud tea and ate the last of my bread, sitting in the sun in front of the cabin. I figured I could wait round most of the morning and still make it home for supper, if I went back a more direct way than I'd come.

When it drew near noon and Bill Jenkins still hadn't shown himself, I figured it was time to head out. Waiting for him had been a long shot, but I hadn't minded. Maybe it had just been an excuse to sit in the sun and let my mind go slack.

What I hadn't noticed, down in that steep-sided valley where the cabin sat, was that the weather was changing.

An hour or so past noon, I reached the top of the ridge from which I'd figured to get a sight of the way home. It was smack dab in the middle of a cloud. A thick, cold, and utterly opaque cloud. I couldn't see a quarter mile, let alone all the way back to Skunk Corners.

Now, if I'd been smart, I'd have turned right around and headed back for the cabin, where there was a fire and maybe even a can of beans. I don't know why I didn't.

Well, I do know. I didn't turn around because I wanted a real meal, from Annie's kitchen. And real coffee, not pine-bud tea. And I figured I knew plenty about these mountains where I'd lived all my life. So I took a deep breath and plunged off in the direction I believed would take me home.

I am not a complete idiot. I had hiked these hills for years, and I had a coat and a bit of food still. I knew how to start a fire at need.

But my coat wasn't waterproof, I'd never been in that exact valley before, and my skills with flint and tinder ended when they got wet.

So, several hours of wandering found me huddled in a shallow cave—more of an overhang, really—cold and damp and gnawing a bit of stale bread and watching the light fade. I'd just begun to cuss myself out for a fool when I realized I wasn't alone.

The man who stood looking at me appeared to be about two years older than the hills, and wore a mix of homespun and hides, but he had a friendly, if quizzical, smile.

"Evening is coming on, and you'll be more comfortable if you come in, rather than sitting here."

I could see no sign of anywhere to come in to, but I followed him anyway, because I'd nothing better to do, and because any promise of being warm and dry was better than what I had now. He led me around a bulge in the cliff and disappeared into the solid wall.

When I stepped up behind him I saw a narrow gap, well hid but big enough to let me pass. Beyond was a nicely furnished cave, slightly smoky from the fire burning below a hole in the ceiling.

Well. I'd found someone living in these hills, and he sure as shootin' wasn't Bill Jenkins.

While the strange little man built up his fire and cut the plants he carried into a soup pot, he introduced himself. Seemed his name was Wes, and he'd come out here a long way back just to learn how the Indians lived in these hills. He'd meant to go back East and write an important paper on it.

"But what with one thing and another, I never got around to it. Just never left," he concluded, filling my tin mug with stew.

I did some thinking while I ate. Partly, I thought about how much I wanted to learn what he knew, because that stew was good. And partly, I thought that if anyone knew where Bill Jenkins was, it'd be this Wes character. Just as I was wondering how to ask, he answered both my questions at once.

"Only thing I missed up here was my students. I used to be a teacher, and it's not so much fun knowing things and having no one to teach. Then last fall I found a young fellow who'd moved up here, to think, he said. He's been a good student."

"So's his son," I said without thinking.

"Hey? What's that?"

"You found Bill Jenkins, didn't you? I'm out looking for him, because I'm his son's teacher and little Billy needs his Pa."

Wes held very still. "That's him. But he said he had no family."

"Then he lied," I said. "I can see him leaving his wife, because she's a drunkard and cantankerous as the devil himself. But his little boy is a sweet child. You take me to him and I'll tell Bill Jenkins what's what."

"Well." Wes had lost his smile completely. "Maybe."

We sat in silence and stared at the fire.

"Well," he said again a few minutes later. "In the morning I'll show you the way to Skunk Corners. That is where you're headed, right?"

I nodded.

"Then I'll go talk to Bill. If you don't see either of us, you can come on back up in a week or so, if you can do it without getting lost."

I'd have liked to have resented that, but given how he'd found me, I didn't figure I had the right.

"And if you're good,' he added, the smile back on his face and in his voice, "I'll teach you what you want to know about these hills."

I figured he must've read my mind, because I surely did want to know about those plants he studied. Especially the ones you could eat. For that, I'd even put up with a second teacher as odd and demanding as the first.

Next morning, Wes escorted me down to the ridge by the windmill. I'd told him I was completely able to find my own way home, now I could see again, but he'd insisted on escorting me practically to my door.

While I scrambled the rest of the way down to town, I tried to convince myself my trip had been a success. After all, my questions had mostly been answered. I just had a whole slew of new ones.

13 THE NINJA LIBRARIAN AND THE NOT-SO-GLORIOUS FOURTH

I might've died of embarrassment about getting lost on the mountain, but I didn't get a chance. I was just too busy to drop dead just then. Anyway, thanks to the Ninja Librarian, no one knew.

See, the Ninja Librarian went and taught those kids from Endoline Monday, and pretended he'd been meant to all along. He told them I had to be away, nothing else.

Sometimes, he's most as good to me as Pa was.

It was almost the Fourth and we all hoped to reproduce the splendiferous event we'd had last year. Especially the picnic. And I wanted to know what Mrs. Herberts would have to say. Tess had somehow talked her into speaking for the women. Tess can talk just about anyone into just about anything, I reckon, though she's yet to talk me into a dress.

The mayor would speak too, of course. You couldn't shut him up, except maybe with a skunk. I thought about finding one to do the job, but at this point, the less I had to do with skunks, the better. And no one would be listening to him anyway, not if we had enough pie. Thanks to Peggy's questions, I wondered about him, despite myself. What right *did* he have to be in charge?

Janey and Joey were reciting. Janey I was sure of, but with Joey I could only cross my fingers and hope for the best. Tommy was coaching him, and if only he didn't panic he'd do well enough. If he did panic, just about anything might come out of his mouth.

But unless it cooled off considerable, there'd be no foot races. The cloud that had enveloped me on the mountain a few days earlier had done little to cool the town, and Peggy and Tommy both declared they weren't going to kill themselves in the heat to prove they were still the fastest. I kind of hoped they'd change their minds, because I thought Peg might win this year. She'd grown over the winter and was all legs, though she'd lost none of her wildness. Tommy could use the defeat, in my opinion. He was getting a bit cocky and superior, as so many boys seem to do around his age.

I taught my six boys and four girls from Endoline, and Franny took up residence in Two-Timin' Tess's Tavern, earning her keep by sweeping up and keeping an eye on Billy when she wasn't in class. And we all got ready for the Fourth.

Hank and Yance were not only building the platform for the Fourth of July speeches, but Tom had somehow gotten the town to pay them. They were so proud of those few dollars they looked fit to bust. I knew how they felt. Getting those boys skilled work with their hands had been the best thing I'd done as their teacher. They even came and asked me to make sure their figures were right, and they were.

I saw nothing of Jake and Harry that week, and I saw neither hide nor hair of either the mysterious Wes nor of Bill Jenkins. After the Fourth, I'd have to go back up the mountain.

In all the excitement, I failed to so much as pick up that Advanced Algebra book.

For all that, I didn't forget to wonder about Tess and how she supported her home for the waifs of the world. Was I one of them? I paid for my meals, mostly, but I wasn't sure that was enough. How much was she charging for the alleged whiskey she sold, anyway? Since I never touched the stuff, I had no idea, but surely not enough to support six, and now eight, people.

She'd made it clear that the obvious answer wasn't right, so I was left thinking about a gold mine. Maybe she'd gotten Bill Jenkins to go up and work one for her. The thought made me laugh. There was no gold up there—and if there was, Tess wasn't crazy enough to trust Jake's brother to mine it.

The Fourth dawned clear and warm, with a promise of greater heat to come, to my sorrow. Maybe we could muster a thunderstorm to cool things down. But then we'd have a soggy picnic. I resigned myself to no races and a lot of sweat.

I went off to the bathhouse in a less cheery mood than usual, but at least the water I'd run into the tub last night—too hot then to touch—was cool and refreshing. Cooler than I was, or would be, anyway. I refilled the tub after my bath. I might want another later.

This year, I was bringing something to the picnic. I'd taken a cookery book from the library, determined to learn to make something fit to eat. My initial notion had run to fried chicken and yeast rolls, but a little reading convinced me to start with a potato salad. Biscuits might've been easier, but I have no oven, and though the heat in my room was fierce, it wasn't quite up to baking bread.

I made a potato salad every day for the four days leading up to the Fourth. The first batch I had to dispose of down the privy, and even there it raised a funny smell. But the second was good enough for Tess's chickens, and the last two I managed to eat. Gradually I came to understand that the measurements in the cookery book had some meaning, and I'd best learn what it was.

By ten a.m. on the Fourth, I had a potato salad which wouldn't kill anyone, though no one would mistake it for Annie's.

As I'd expected, I also needed another bath. Cooking's hot work, at least for me.

Tom had been and gone in the meantime, using up the water I'd run into the tub, but the liquid that gushed out of the pipe was still pleasantly cool.

By the time I finished in the bathhouse, people were starting to gather. The races should've been under way, but it seemed everyone agreed with Tommy and Peg—too hot to run. We'd go straight to the picnic and the speeches. Folks were hauling the tables out of Tess's and Mrs. Herberts' places to set up in the bit of dirt we called the Town Square. There was less shade there than there'd been a year ago, thanks to the big storm, which had knocked the best shade tree onto Tess's barroom. I'd need a hat to sit out there, so I dug around and found Pa's old hat. It was dirty and stained, but it kept the sun off.

It was also about the only thing I had that'd belonged to Pa.

Equipped for the day, I headed around back of Tess's for the extra planks we'd used as benches the previous year, only to realize that they weren't there. We'd used all the spare lumber and then some in rebuilding the Tavern.

Now what? The tables and chairs from the Tavern and Tea Shop wouldn't seat a quarter of us, not to mention we'd need a place to set all the food.

For now, I put my potato salad in the library basement where it was cool. I sniffed when I went in—Tom was cooking something I couldn't identify. I tried to remember if I'd ever noticed him cooking before. But I couldn't even recall if, before he'd gone away, I'd even seen him eating, let alone cooking. Well, he'd eaten a little at last year's picnic. Whatever else he'd eaten back then, he'd done it in private. Now he came to Annie's kitchen nearly every night, same as me. Once I even saw him munching sandwiches at the Tea Shop. He was chatting with Mrs. Holstead and tickling young James Thomas's toes.

Something had definitely changed Tom while he was away. I determined to learn what, just as soon as I found Bill Jenkins and figured out how Tess kept her tavern afloat.

Meanwhile, we had a picnic to run. Tess pointed me in the direction of the mercantile, where Mr. Johnson had laid a stack of boards on the porch. Hank and Yance were there with Ike Holstead, building sawhorses. I carried a few pair over to the square and came back for planks, then set the whole thing up where Tess told me to.

Seeing Tess directing things turned my mind to another issue, and I looked around for Mayor Burton. There he was, fussing over the bunting the women draped on the speaking platform. No one paid him much mind. Mrs. Herberts seemed to be in charge there.

Maybe Peggy was right. Certainly Mr. Burton didn't make for much of a mayor. But if we needed a new one, it looked to me like our real leaders were the women. I knew who'd have my vote.

Except I wasn't allowed to vote, not even now that I'd turned eighteen. Women, it seemed, could do darn near anything, but we couldn't vote and we couldn't declare right out we were in charge.

I couldn't wait to hear what Mrs. Herberts would speak on.

I was doomed not to find out. At least we got most of the way through lunch before disaster struck. Mrs. Holstead even told me my potato salad was quite good, though she might've been lying, on account of I'd just told her what a smart girl and great help Janey was. I'm starting to figure out how the world works.

Anyway, I'd just taken my first bite of pie—a work of art Annie had baked to perfection—when trouble rode into town.

A dozen or more rough men from Endoline.

I knew they were from Endoline, because I recognized some of them. One in particular I had extra cause to hate.

That kind of hate is first cousin to fear. I hung back behind the crowd, which gave me a chance to see how others in our community responded to the invasion.

"Mayor" Burton took one look and sort of faded into the woodwork.

Several other men, including Mr. Holstead, moved closer to their families.

Mrs. Herberts and Annie planted themselves in front of the food table, ready to defend their pies by whatever means necessary. I liked their priorities.

Tess, Mr. Johnson from the Mercantile, Jake, Harry, and the Ninja Librarian all moved forward, from different parts of the crowd, to confront the invaders.

I saw Johnny step out of the Tavern, where he'd just begun serving well-watered drinks. I noticed he was holding the shotgun he kept under the bar. I'd never before seen him so much as touch the thing.

The toughs didn't see Johnny. They were kind of focused on Tom and Tess, whom they sized up with a kind of sneer.

"Look, Mort," said a fellow whose name I couldn't recall. "Just like we heard. This town's *defended*"—he put a world of contempt into the word—"by an old man and a tavern wench."

I heard a low growl from the crowd. Folks here didn't like some outsider calling Tess names. Not even the ones who didn't approve of Tess or her Tavern.

"We've come for our young 'uns," Mort announced. "You've got my Benny, and Pete's Frannie, and you've been filling their heads with nonsense."

That was when I remembered that I didn't have to be afraid of Mortimer Black any more. I wasn't a scared girl now, but a grown-up with some decent Ninja moves in her.

"Only an idiot like you, Mort Black, would think education is nonsense. Maybe if there was a little more of that 'nonsense' up there in Endoline, a decent person would consider staying more than five minutes."

He looked at me, and he knew me, all right. His lip started to curl, and he opened his mouth.

I really didn't want him to say aloud what I could read on his face, so I just reached out a hand

and tipped him off that horse. Since he'd slung one leg around the saddle horn, it was easy to do.

Old Mort hit the ground with a thump they could probably hear up in Endoline, and all heck broke loose.

The rest of Mortimer Black's companions rode around him and came straight for me. Since none stopped to see if Mort was alive or dead, I guessed they weren't so much interested in him as they were looking for an excuse to cut loose.

I wasn't quite sure how to address a herd of charging horsemen, so I took a quick look to see what the Ninja Librarian was doing.

He was diving out of the way.

I did the same, and the whole crowd split to let them through. That left only the pie table in their way, and my heart sank.

You know, those horses must've been stolen, because they had more manners than their riders. Every one of them leapt right over that board, and when they began to mill on the other side, Tom and I went into action.

Before we had done more than take a few steps towards the horsemen, Johnny went into action and brought everything to a halt. He fired off that old shotgun over everyone's heads, and it was loud enough to get their attention.

In the moment of silence that followed the blast, Tess's voice rang out.

"Get out, or get down and have some pie. We'll have no brawls here."

The roughs looked a little lost without their leader, who was just sitting up and looking around as though he wasn't sure where he was. His horse had high-tailed it for home, which like I said probably wasn't Mort's place.

Crazy Jake Jenkins and Wild Harry Colsen picked up Mort from both sides and called out to the still-hesitating horsemen, "Come an' take him home, or we'll toss him in the jail for disturbin' the peace."

Skunk Corners didn't have a jail, nor a sheriff to run it, but they didn't have to know that.

Alas, the Endoline outlaws got down, but they didn't come in peaceful. Nor did they stop to eat any pie, which just proves they weren't very bright.

The women ran for cover, the kids ran for the pies, and the rest of us dove into what might've been the biggest Fourth of July brawl in the history of our mountain, if not the nation.

We were a bit outnumbered, by the time the mayor and some of the others had followed the women and children out of the square—to protect them, of course.

But we had a Ninja and a half on our side—I figure I made about half the fighter Tom did—and while they were huntin' trouble, we were defending our town.

And, oddly, we were defending *their* children.

When the dust settled, we loaded every one of those men onto their horses (save for Mort, of course; his horse being long gone, he had to share a saddle with the smallest of his cronies). Then we smacked those beasts on the rumps and off they went.

I hoped the horses would carry the men back to where they'd been stolen.

Then we took stock. Our speakers' platform was a wreck, every one of us was broken or bleeding somewhere—and the kids had eaten the last of the pie.

I dabbed at a cut over my left eye with my right hand, while Tess wrapped my rapidly swelling left wrist and stuck it into a sling.

Even Tom had a bloody nose, and Harry and

Jake were pretty battered, with matching black eyes that weren't going to go over so well when they went back to work in the morning. But no one was killed or even much maimed.

In my eyes, the worst of it was the pie I didn't get to eat. Those youngsters would hear plenty from me about that. And I was sorry I didn't get to hear the speeches.

"Well!" said Mrs. Herberts. "I think that was enough excitement for one day. I'm going in for a nice cup of tea."

Heads nodded and people gathered up what they could find of their belongings.

I found myself cornered by Tess and Tom, both looking grave.

"Why, Al? Why'd you start it?"

"You deliberately provoked that battle, Alice. That is most unlike you, and I would like to know the reason."

They deserved an answer if anyone did, but I just couldn't give it. I had vowed not to think about my life in Endoline, and I wasn't going to change that now.

Since lying never did me any good with those two, I just said, "I had to," and limped off to my room.

They could make up their own answers to that question. My answers were sealed inside where they'd never get out.

14 THE NINJA LIBRARIAN AND THE LOGGERS

Two days after the Fourth, I headed back up into the hills. My wrist was still swollen and sore, but I kept it in the sling and headed out anyway. It would be an easy walk. I knew where I was going this time, and I had no intention of getting lost.

Nor did I. I reached Wes's cave well before noon. Only trouble was, it wasn't there. I knew I was in the right spot, and even found the marks where I'd built myself a bit of a shelter before he found me.

What I couldn't do was find the opening to that cave.

In the end, I had to stand near where I thought it should be, feeling like an idiot, and yell, "Hey, Mr. Wes! It's Big Al! Can I come in?" I figured that way, any answer would tell me where to go and I could just pretend I was being polite but knew where he was all along.

It didn't work. No one answered.

Naturally. He was probably out somewhere doing whatever he did up here. I thought about hiking on over to see if Bill Jenkins was at the cabin, but didn't want to go that far. My wrist throbbed now with every step, and my head ached, along with some other parts that hadn't come off so well in the fight.

In the end, I wrote a note using a pencil stub and a scrap of paper I found in my pocket.

Wes, I wanted to see you and maybe Bill. Billy's still waiting. Big Al.

Then I had to figure out where to leave the note. After some thought, I stuck it on a branch stub near where I knew that entrance must be, and I headed back down the mountain.

I was nearly back to Skunk Corners when I heard noises I didn't expect. Axes and saws. Was someone clearing land, or getting some firewood in? No one had said anything about either task, and one thing our town's good at is minding each others' business.

This called for a closer look.

I chose to take my look from somewhere out of sight, just out of habit. That turned out to be a good thing. As I peered from a handy clump of bushes, I realized this was no lone homesteader getting firewood.

It was a full-blown lumber camp, or fast turning into one, and making far too much progress already.

As I turned away, I found myself face to face with the most feared animal on our mountain. But rather than spraying me as I might have deserved, the skunk gave me a look that was just plain pleading. Just one long, desperate look, then the critter waddled back into the woods.

I knew I now had the means to end that feud, if only I could figure out how to stop the loggers.

This was too important to mess up on my own. I mean, finding Billy's Pa, or giving those kids from Endoline maybe the only chance they'd get, those things mattered. But protecting our woods and getting back on the right side of the skunks, that meant the world to me.

I went straight to Tom.

He was out, but a look at the sun told me it was lunchtime, so I headed across to Tess's. He was there, all right, eating lunch with Tess. That was fine, because I wanted her advice too. And lunch.

I told them what I'd seen, and kept an eye on Tess while I told it, just to be sure she didn't already know. I didn't think she'd do that to us but I did need to check, because I knew she was up to something.

"So we have to stop it, right?" I finished. "Besides, if we do, I'm pretty sure we won't have any more trouble with the skunks."

The critters hadn't come into town since Tom ejected the one that sprayed the mayor and his wife, but they still made an evening walk in the woods a chancy thing.

Tom and Tess raised their eyebrows in much the same way, but didn't ask how I knew that, nor did they suggest I was imagining things, the way they once had. I was all the more glad of that, because I knew it was a crazy thought. But the look that skunk had given me. . . I was sure it meant something.

Upshot was, I took them both back up the hill and showed them the lumber camp. Tess's mouth tightened to a line when she saw it, and her glance drifted off to a hillside not far away. I made a note to check over there for the still or the mine or whatever it was Tess kept hidden to finance her Tavern—or the home for waifs of the world it more and more resembled.

But first we had to take care of our little problem.

We considered the layout in silence for some time, then crept back off the ridge and headed to Town without saying anything.

I was pretty sure some of those men were from Endoline. I'd not seen Mort Black, at least, but that didn't mean he wasn't around. And if they were from Endoline, I knew we could be confident they weren't there for anyone's good but their own. Black's own.

I still didn't know what to do. And what if they were there by rights? I'd always thought of the woods as part of the town, but no one owned them.

Did they?

When I asked Tom and Tess, they looked more grave than ever.

"Homesteaders own their claims, of course," Tess said. "But I'm pretty sure no one's staked that side of town."

"Any otherwise unclaimed lands would belong to the government," Tom said.

"Well then." I thought about it. "That means no one should be out there cutting the trees, right?"

"Alas," Tom said. "The government may give permission where it likes."

"Who is this government, and what gives him the right?" I resented the idea. "Seems to me we're the ones should have a say. If anyone's going to cut the trees around our town, it should be us."

"Well," Tom began, but Tess cut him off.

"We should have a say, and so we shall. I don't care who gave permission, if so be it anyone did. We know what those men are doing, and we know why. And we are going to put a stop to it."

Tom closed his mouth and made no further arguments.

Sure we'd stop them. The only question was, how?

Finally, Tom suggested that we should go talk to them, before doing anything else. I thought that was a crazy idea, but Tess went along.

"Not me." I crossed my arms and stuck out my chin. "I am not going to go talk to those, those," I couldn't find a word for that lot, not one I'd say in front of Tom. Instead, I said, "Mort Black is behind it."

"You can't know that," Tess objected.

"I know that he is a low-down, dirty rotten lyin' louse, who hates me and you and anyone who isn't under his thumb!"

They were both looking at me, astonished at my outburst. I turned red.

"We've had words, him and me," I muttered.

Tess gave me a considering sort of look, started to say something, then closed her mouth and nodded, as though she understood something.

I hoped she didn't understand too much.

Well, they went off to the camp, and when they came back, I knew I'd had the rights of it.

"Got nothin' from 'em, did you?"

Tom frowned a little at my abuse of the English language and all that, but all he said was,

"They proved uncooperative."

Yeah, I'd have bet they did!

Looking at them and thinking about our next move, I realized that he and Tess had known before they went that talk was unlikely to succeed. They also knew, though, that if talk didn't do it, odds were things would get ugly.

Sure enough, we were still thinking about what to do next when Tommy and Peggy came in, followed by Hank and Yance.

"Teacher!" Tommy, as always, was first to speak, often without looking or thinking. "There's a bunch a no-goods from Endoline cuttin' our trees!"

"I know."

"So what are you doin' settin' there? You gotta *do* somethin' or come the rains, our spring'll be all full of muck!"

I hadn't thought about that part of it, but he was right. Without trees on that ridge, and the land all torn up, we'd have muck and mud all down our slopes, messing up creek and spring alike.

"I aim to stop them," I assured the kids.

Not such kids anymore, because Peggy fixed me with a too-knowing look and asked, "How?"

Well. Now we were back where we'd been for the last hour.

It took the lot of us—plus Johnny, Tildy, Ike Holstead, and assorted other townsfolk who wandered by—two more hours to figure it out. But when we had our plan, I chuckled a little with satisfaction.

It was dark up on that ridge, among the trees still standing. It didn't help that I still half expected an unpleasant visit from *Mephista mephista*, as my book on "Nature Studies" had said I should call our aromatic friends.

Of course, if skunks did come, it could only help, in this instance.

Two dozen denizens of Skunk Corners— Skunkians? Cornerites?—lurked in the darkest places surrounding the loggers' camp. No lights burned below. It was well into the darkest hours of the night, and even their cook fire, carelessly left burning as they went to sleep, had reduced itself to the barest ruby glimmer.

Down below, Peggy, Tommy, and Annie, the smallest and nimblest of our crew, moved silently between the sleeping forms, collecting axes and saws. It worried me, but they—and Tom—were the quietest among us, so I had to let them do it.

They passed the tools into the darkness, where Tom himself put the next stage of the plan into action.

We'd argued a long time about this part. Easiest would have been to drop the things down a mine shaft, but Ike and Johnny objected to the waste. I could see their point, and Tom came up with the idea he now executed.

At last they finished. As the silent thieves left the camp, Annie lit just one match, and blew it out as soon as it flared.

At that signal, the woods all around the camp came to life with the sounds of every creature of the forest, all angry and annoyed.

Some of us were better at it than others, but the overall effect scared even me. The loggers awoke suddenly and in a bewildered fog, a fog greatly enhanced by the whiskey Johnny had sold the crew after dinner. He hadn't watered those drinks at all.

They groped for the axes that weren't there, and the sounds of their confusion began to rival the "animal" noises.

Finally, someone thought to rekindle the fire, and they gathered around it. Huddled around it, I ought to say. Every time some of them started to look like they might go out and investigate, Yance gave a long wolf howl, or Tess gave her best mountain lion scream.

When the first hint of light touched the sky in the east, we began to trickle back off to town. Some had left earlier, leaving the job to the best howlers and growlers. Most went off to bed for a little sleep. Tom pointed out that I'd missed my lesson the night before, and hauled me off to fix that.

I didn't even try to argue.

Around noon a half-dozen loggers stopped at Two-Timin' Tess's Tavern, on their way to the depot.

"We're closin' it down," one said, a couple of drinks later. "That there wood is ha'nted. Or the critters is, which is even wuss. 'Sides, all our tools vanished. Just up and disappeared right into thin air! No sir, I ain't stickin' around no more."

"A wise move," Johnny assured him. "We have always found it best to avoid that area. The animals—but no, you wouldn't believe me."

"Oh yes, I would," the logger said, as he headed for the door, "I would indeed."

Another logger added, "That fellow from up the line, one who hired us, I noticed he didn't stick around." The train whistled coming into town, and the loggers headed for the depot in a hurry.

A few hours later, Mort Black himself came into town. I wondered at his nerve, but for all that, he had more than I did. I watched from Tess's kitchen, and kept out of his way. If he didn't see me, he wasn't likely to think of saying things I didn't want said.

Mort blustered around a fair bit, trying to accuse the townsfolk of all sorts of things, but Tess, Johnny, and Tom met each accusation with a smooth assurance that we had all been home and abed all night. They even offered that he could search our sheds for the missing tools.

Johnny poured himself an apparently stiff drink. I grinned. He'd served himself from the bottle he kept for me. He knocked it back in a gulp and poured another to give him the courage to say, in a low voice, "That neck of the woods is *trouble*, mister. The critters. . . I dunno, but you wouldn't catch me doin' much of anything there."

Tess just happened to be nearby. She nodded solemnly. "The skunks, especially."

No one could have missed the fact that Mort had been too close and cozy with a skunk, and recently. He scowled, but a subtle movement on Tom's part reminded him how his last attempt to throw his weight around in Skunk Corners had ended, and soon he was hiking up the trail back to Endoline. He didn't seem to have a horse.

I wasn't sure we'd seen the last of that low-down snake, but I didn't think he'd try logging our woods again.

I joined the others, and Johnny poured me a slug of the strong tea I always drank.

By the next day they were all gone, and only their mess remained when Tom and I took the young folks out to collect the tools they'd hidden high in the trees. We'd have to clean the place up, but for now we enjoyed our victory.

"I have found," Tom explained, as he pointed out what seemed to be in plain sight, "that very few people look up, even when searching for something."

Now, that gave me an idea. I'd a hunch the librarian had just answered another question.

15 THE NINJA LIBRARIAN LEAVES IT TO AL

When a week had gone by and we'd seen neither hide nor hair of any troublemakers from Endoline, I decided it was time to get back to Bill Jenkins. I'd not seen hide nor hair of him, either. School would start soon, and then I wouldn't be free to roam the hills. Of course, I had Ryan and his friends to think about now, but I had an idea about that.

I knew it was a good idea, but it wasn't easy to convince Ryan.

"I can't do that, Teacher! They'll think I think I'm better 'n them!"

I refrained from pointing out that, at least in terms of learning and probably smarts, he is better. It wouldn't help.

"I'm the teacher, and I say you can and you will. What's more," I took a deep breath and went on, figuring I might as well get it all over with at once, "when my regular school starts up and you all can't come down here all the time, you will keep right on teaching them."

That floored him so completely he couldn't even speak, so I went on writing him out a lesson plan.

It took two days to convince him, but when I headed back up the mountain after Billy's Pa, Ryan was standing at my desk, face white as the stripe on a skunk, instructing his former classmates to open their readers.

Tom lurked in the cloakroom to offer help if needed. He and I had talked it all over and figured it never hurt to be prepared. Not that he'd be needed. I knew, even if Ryan didn't, that his friends knew darn well he was way ahead of them in schoolwork. And, since he'd got them all to come to Skunk Corners and ask me to teach them, they already saw him as their leader.

Ryan would be fine. I put him and the students out of my mind as I climbed the ridge. I was headed to Wes's cave first thing. I'd go on to Bill Jenkins's cabin at the mine if I had to, but I hoped I wouldn't. It was hot, and I was losing my temper with that man. An extra tramp three miles cross-country wouldn't make me any nicer. My wrist was mostly better, but using it to catch trees and balance myself over rough ground made it ache, and that made me grumpy.

When I got near the cave, I followed the advice Tom hadn't known he'd given me, and looked up. Sure enough, there was the smoke rising from an invisible gap in the rocks, a little south of where I'd expected it.

After that, it was easy to follow my nose, and my ears. Two men were in there, cooking some kind of meat over the fire, and talking.

I didn't stop to knock and be polite. I just stepped inside, faced Bill Jenkins, and let him have it. I will not tell you exactly what I said, because I'm a little ashamed now.

Only a little, mind, especially since it worked. But I'd better not repeat it all.

I just told he had as fine a little son as a man could want, and that if he put me off again and didn't come right now to see the boy, I'd know him for the coward he gave every appearance of being. I went on for several minutes, being a little worked up after stewing over it all the way from town, not to mention during all those other tramps about the mountains searching for the man. Both of them just stared at me with their mouths open.

By the time I finished, Mr. Jenkins' face was as red as my long winter underwear, and he closed his mouth slowly. Seemed he couldn't meet my eyes, because he kept looking at the meat sizzling over the fire, like somehow it could tell him what to do.

Wes was looking at me, though, and I couldn't tell if the gleam in his eye was amusement or encouragement or just reflected light. At this point, I didn't care.

"Well?" I prodded. Standing in the entrance to that cave home, hands on hips and glaring, I probably looked outlandish. Maybe even scary.

I hoped I did.

Bill still didn't speak, so I walked over and nudged him with my toe.

"Well?"

At last he looked at me.

"I didn't know," he muttered.

"You didn't know," I echoed. "You didn't know you had a little boy? You didn't know he looks up to you as the greatest thing since apple pie? Or did you fail to notice you left him behind when you walked out without a word?"

At least that shook him out of his inability to

speak.

"I didn't *know*," he emphasized, "if I had a son at all."

It took me a moment to understand. When I did, I didn't think much of his answer.

"Six years you're his Pa. Only Pa he knows of or—for whatever unfathomable reason—wants. I say nothing else matters, that makes him your son. From the looks of things, a better son than you deserve. But for some reason he wants you back, so are you coming?"

I crossed my arms and tapped my foot, exactly the way I once saw Mrs. Mayor Burton doing when she didn't get fast enough service from Mr. Johnson at the Mercantile.

To my surprise, it worked. Bill Jenkins stood up and looked at old Wes, who nodded.

"Al is spot on, I'd say. Wherever he sprung from, the sprout is yours." He turned to me. "As for you, Al, I will see you this evening by the windmill. There are things it's time you learned."

It was my turn to be red. I hoped he was talking about plants, but I wasn't sure. He certainly didn't sound quite so lost in his own botanical world as I'd thought he'd be.

He sounded, in fact, a lot like the Ninja Librarian. I had a hunch I was in for a world of trouble.

While we talked, Bill Jenkins had picked up his hat and coat and started for the door, so I just nodded at Wes and followed.

Once outside, Bill stopped.

"One thing, Big Al. I will not go back to that viper I married."

"I wouldn't ask it." I wanted nothing to do with Ina Jenkins, nor her brother, Cal Potts. "Billy's living with Tess these days."

"At the Tavern?" His frown deepened.

"Where he has five—six, now—mothers who all dote on him. For a while, I thought it might be enough. But he wants his Pa."

"So you're bringing me in." His smile was wry, but it was a smile and improved his looks—and my opinion of him.

"Yup."

"What do you want me to do?"

"Dunno. You'll have to figure that out yourself. Maybe it's enough to come into town and see him regular. Maybe not."

"I've got a job to do up there." He tipped his head to indicate the mountain. "I can't just walk away."

"You'll figure it out," I repeated. I thought maybe it was time to give him some encouragement, having blown him up so thoroughly. I'd ask about that job later, though.

He nodded and said nothing more until we reached the edge of town. There he suddenly stopped.

Bill Jenkins had been red-faced when we left Wes's cave, but he was pale now.

"I can't just walk in there and see him in front of everybody."

I thought about that. There might be some sticky emotions. I could understand him not wanting to meet his son in front of the regulars at the Tavern.

I looked around. It was only just past noon. The kids were still at the school. My room wouldn't be very private, given the thin walls. That left the library.

"Okay. I'll let you in the back of the library, into Tom's rooms, then bring Billy over."

It was a good plan, but things don't always work according to plans.

We were crossing the street between the school and the library, hurrying to get out of sight, when we heard a yell that stopped us in our tracks.

"Pa!"

A blur flew past me and Billy launched himself into his father's arms, near knocking them both sprawling.

"Pa, Pa, I knew Teacher would find you!" Billy was hugging his Pa so tight it half strangled him, but Bill made no move to dislodge the boy.

When I realized they were both crying, I grabbed Bill's arm and hustled them around the corner of the library and into the woodshed, that being the closest private spot.

Then I shut the door and went to stand guard. Maybe I wiped away a tear or two myself. Just because I'm Big Al doesn't mean I don't have feelings.

What they said was no business of mine, nor anyone else. Though I was dying to know, I beat back my curiosity. My job was just to make sure they got it all said with no interruptions. In this town, that might take some work.

The first to come was Franny, since she'd have been watching Billy when he flew off across the street. She panted up as soon as I'd shut the door on the Jenkins men.

"Oh! Teacher! What—?" she gasped, out of breath, unable to finish her question.

I took her arm and led her away from the shed. "Billy's Pa's come back. I guess Billy saw him. I was going to come get him when Mr. Jenkins was inside."

"Oh!" Franny clapped her hands. "That's just wonderful! Billy's been wanting him so."

By the time she finished this speech, Tess had arrived, as had half a dozen of my regular students, who'd been inside the library and heard the commotion.

Some were in favor of rushing right in to congratulate Billy. I planted myself in front of the crowd and growled.

"You all get out of here and leave them two alone. First one to go past me gets kicked into the middle of next week."

I must've looked like I meant it, because they left in a hurry. The children returned to the library, and the adults to Two-Timin' Tess's Tavern. No doubt both places would be abuzz with the sensation for hours.

Only Tess remained when all the scurrying ceased.

"What now, Alice? Is he coming home? Did he say what he's been doing up there?"

I was looking right at her, or I might have thought she just wanted to know what would happen to Billy now. But I saw the flash of relief when I said, "I don't know. He said he has a job up there, and he didn't know just what to do about Billy." I watched carefully while I said it, and I would swear Bill Jenkin's job up on the mountain wasn't any surprise to her.

Tess knew something about him, and I wanted to know what.

When Billy and his Pa finally came out of that woodshed, I was sitting on the library steps, getting Tom's report on Ryan's first day as a teacher. As I'd hoped and expected, it had gone well, and Tom had never come out of hiding.

"He did appear moderately nervous, but the other children were patient and respectful," he was saying, when the Jenkins men came around the corner.

"Ah, um, glad you're here, Al. We need to talk

about—" He nodded at his son.

"We'll want to include Tess," I said, and watched him for a reaction. Something about his look told me that he and Tess shared a secret.

"We'll want Tom, too," I added as I stood.

"No, Alice, I believe that this time I will leave it to you."

Well. Seemed to me this one could use all the brains we could find, but when I looked at Tom, he just shook his head.

"I have a library full of children in need of an adult," he said, and went back inside. For whatever reason, he didn't want to help with this problem. If he had, he'd have left the kids in an instant.

With a shrug, I turned to follow Bill and Billy across the street.

"So, Bill, you're working for Tess?" I made it somewhere between a question and a statement.

It worked. He glanced from me to the Tavern and said, "Least said about that the better."

I had another bit of the story.

When we got to the Tavern, Franny took Billy off to fill the kindling baskets, and we settled into a parley in the kitchen.

Only then did it hit me. I looked at Tess.

"You knew." This time my anger was the cold kind. "You knew all along just where he was, and you never said. Not even with Billy right here and wanting his Pa."

"Yes." Just that one word, and I was all ready to lay into her, but Tess had more to say.

"I'm sorry. I was protecting—things—and I made the wrong choice." She looked from Bill to me and back. "I was going to tell you, Bill, the next time I went up there. About Billy."

"But Al got there first." He sighed. "I don't

reckon you'd have been as convincing."

I turned red, remembering what I'd said to him.

"Right." Tess was all business again. "It does leave us with a dilemma."

"Is it a mine or a still," I interrupted. I was tired of half-truths and talking around things. I wanted to know exactly what was going on.

Tess sighed. "Does it matter?"

"It might." Either one could spell trouble, but different kinds of trouble we'd have to meet in different ways. Anyway, I wanted to know. I sat and glared at them.

Bill gave in first. "Both."

"It's like this," Tess said. "I've had a still up yonder for years, brewing my own brand of drink, and it's less nasty that what I can buy. Last winter the fellow who tended it for me quit in a huff and went off to the city. I ran it myself for a while, but it was tough. Then one day I met Bill up there."

"I'd gone off to think things over, after Ina— never mind that," he said. "When Tess asked if I'd stay on a bit and take care of things, it seemed like a good idea."

"And then he found some color, not in the old mine, but gold flakes in the stream."

"Not much," Bill added, "but enough to make a difference. So I stayed."

I digested this. Tess needed someone up there, no question. And the fewer folks knew what Tess had, the better. But Billy needed his Pa.

"It's no place for a child," Bill said.

There were those who said the Tavern was no place for a child, either. But we all knew they were wrong about that. Yet Billy did need his Pa.

I could ask Tom for help, but he'd tossed this back in my lap and no way out of it. Again I wondered why. Did he not want to know what Tess was up to?

"I think we need a compromise," I said. "Bill goes on with what he's doing, only he comes into town regular, and takes Billy up there from time to time. Billy goes on living here, mostly, and especially when the weather gets bad. And would Wes maybe help with the still so you could get away more? He knows plants and all."

"It just might work," Bill allowed after some thought. "If I had some help, I could come to town some."

We had to explain Wes to Tess, and he did take some explaining. But in the end, she agreed to try. He seemed unlikely to turn her in to any higher authority, if he even acknowledged any, which didn't seem likely.

So Billy had his Pa, Bill had his job—well away from his regrettable wife—and Tess had her income.

Only question I had left was why Tom had left it all to me. I never did figure that out.

16 THE NINJA LIBRARIAN AND THE FOREST FIRE

It had been quiet in Skunk Corners for a few weeks, and I got antsy, thinking too much. Ryan was teaching up in Endoline—and coming down to ask for help and advice lots of evenings, which gave me a chance to help him along in his own studies, too. My own students were back in school, and sometimes even working hard. Billy and his Pa were figuring out their new way of living.

Like I say, everything was pretty quiet. We hadn't even seen anything of Ina Jenkins, which worried me some. I had no wish to see her, to be sure, but I couldn't help worrying that she'd come back for Billy, and maybe with more help. Her brother Cal Potts no doubt had friends just like him, down in Two-Bit.

I'd have to handle that when and if it happened. To take my mind off things I couldn't change, including wondering what Mort Black might get up to next, I decided it was time to learn more about the Ninja Librarian's past. I wanted to know why he'd really left us—and why he came back.

So, like a fool as I often am, I just up and asked him. Now, some would say you should always just be direct, and I do usually take a straight line toward where I'm going. But some things need a different touch, and I had to learn that the hard way. So I up and asked.

"I do not think you need to know that."

"Oh, come on." He'd changed enough since coming back that I thought I could wheedle. "I just want to know how someone becomes a Ninja Librarian." I remembered that once he'd sort of hinted that there'd been a school or something.

Instead of answering, Tom put me through an extra hour of fighting practice. Thanks to that, I was late getting up to the windmill to meet Wes, and he kept me working so long I learned to identify three plants in the dark by smell alone.

Sometimes I wondered if those two were getting together to figure out ways to make me suffer.

Anyway, once I'd brought it up, I couldn't seem to let go of the idea that Tom owed me some explanations. He made it clear he didn't agree, but I persisted. I kept narrowing my questions, until I settled on one which, I vowed, I would ask until he answered it.

"Who said you had to leave us?"

I figured that would give me something to go on, if he'd only answer it.

I figured if I asked it often enough, he'd get tired of dodging the question. What could it hurt if he told?

I still don't know what it would hurt if he told, but I finally learned what it would hurt if I kept asking.

That was how I came to be wandering the hills on a hot September afternoon, instead of taking my usual lesson in the cool of the library basement. When I arrived and asked my question for the tenth time, Tom lost his temper.

I hadn't even known he could do that.

Anyway, he told me to get out and stay out until I learned proper respect for my teacher and my elders. I'm sort of summarizing here. He offered more details.

I left fast, before I could call him a cantankerous old son of a grizzly. So you see, I did one smart thing. Thanks to that, I left under my own power, which was something, anyway.

Since I was mad enough to bite the heads off nails, let alone anyone who spoke to me, I headed for the hills to cool off. Cool my temper, I mean. The rest of me got plenty hot, climbing that mountain.

I made it all the way to the top of Skunk Mountain before I stopped stewing and realized it was getting dark.

Well. Now I could choose to sleep on the summit and be late for school in the morning, or I could spend the night climbing down in the dark.

I'd not taken a thing with me when I stormed out of the library, so I couldn't have built a fire even if there'd been any wood up there, which there wasn't. I didn't have a coat or anything. It would be a long, cold night if I stayed, this high up and coming on toward fall.

With a sigh, and blaming Tom every step of the way, I started down, my eyes straining to pick the way in the gathering darkness.

It should have been a moonlit night, but clouds had come up in the afternoon, and I'd heard thunder from time to time. I did hope it would rain soon, but not that night.

Even with the clouds, it wasn't too hard to pick my way down from the bald summit to the edge of the trees. But after that, it got a lot worse, and I don't much like to think of that hike. The storm had moved closer, and lightning and thunder disrupted the night, though the rain held off.

About halfway down I smelled smoke. I was deep in the forest by then and couldn't see a thing, but there'd been lightning, and I knew that somewhere out there something must be smoldering. It gave me a powerful urge to hurry. That gave me a whole new fit of rage at the Ninja Librarian, because I couldn't move any faster. Not if I didn't want to break a leg and lie out there until the lions ate me and the coyotes crunched my bones.

By the time I reached town, the storm had moved on and the setting moon shone out beneath the clouds. Of course, me being under the trees and the moon above them, it didn't do me much good.

I was still in a rotten mood, so I cussed the whole outfit—town, moon, and mountain—pretty good before I reached home.

It must've been an hour or so before dawn, and all I wanted was to fall into bed and sleep. Trouble was, that smoke I'd smelled hadn't gone away. It drifted over the town in a thickening cloud, and that meant trouble.

I headed for the library, then stopped in the middle of the street and reconsidered. I turned to the Tavern instead.

It wasn't Tom I wanted this time, nor even Tess. It was Johnny. Of all the men who lived in town, he struck me as the most level-headed and practical. The Ninja Librarian was smart, but he wasn't always practical. And he wasn't brought up in these mountains.

If that lightning had started a fire anywhere near town, we'd need someone whose common sense couldn't be upended.

Johnny slept in a loft over the woodshed. Used to be he only slept there in warm weather, moving to the barroom come winter, but when we rebuilt the shed after the tree squashed it, we made it tight and put in a stove. Not that he'd needed one yet, but seemed to me Johnny deserved that much, and Tess didn't argue. Besides, I'd salvaged the stove from an abandoned mine cabin, so it didn't cost anything but some trouble.

Now I headed around the Tavern right to the shed. We'd have to wake the others soon enough, if it really was a fire. Johnny could help me figure out if we had trouble or not.

When I reached the woodshed, I stopped. I couldn't just go charging up into his room. What if he didn't wear a nightshirt in hot weather? What if he took his shotgun to bed?

I stood at the foot of his ladder and hollered, "Johnny!"

I called two or three times before I heard feet hit the floor. A sleepy and irritated voice hollered back, "What?"

"It's me. Big Al. Johnny, we've maybe got trouble."

"Do I come armed?" He sounded more awake and less irritated.

"Not shooting trouble. But maybe a fire."

I heard a muffled sound that was probably cussing, and he practically slid down the ladder. His shirt was in his hand, but his pants and boots were in order. He pulled the shirt on while I explained—about the storm and the smoke, not the reason I was up on the mountain in the middle of the night.

I didn't really need to say much. The smoke was thick enough now to be obvious.

"Have you spotted the fire?"

"No. But—it's gotta be down the mountain from us. I've been on the ridge, and it's not up that way."

Downhill from town was bad. Fires like to run uphill.

"We need to wake the town. Any kids who can ride for the nearby farms?"

"Janey, Joey, and Lije. Maybe Sarah. The rest are either too little or live out of town." I didn't mention MaryBeth Burton. Her parents would never let her go.

"Send 'em. Steal horses if you have to. I'll wake the menfolk and Tess."

Now I wanted Tom, forgetting I was mad at him, but the Ninja Librarian would have to wait. Getting those kids off to warn the farms—or call on their help if they were out of the fire's way—was more important.

It took less than half an hour to get my messengers on their way. By then it was getting almost light enough to make out the trail.

When I'd seen the kids off and returned to Tess's, everyone in town was up and most were at the Tavern. The Ninja Librarian was there, without his frock coat and with a serious expression on his face.

He also seemed to have forgotten our fight. He took me aside to whisper, "Alice, do you know how serious this may be? I know nothing of wildfires." And there wasn't time to read up on them, I thought.

"We won't know until we get enough light to see it. At least there's no flames in sight. That has to be a good thing."

From his look, I think he guessed that I didn't know all that much about fires, either.

"Mr. Tom!" Johnny's orders cut off our discussion. "Go fill that bathtub of yours, and when it's full, start filling washtubs. Mrs. Herberts, you have the women haul those tubs and soak every roof in town."

That made sense. I looked around. My older students were gone down the trails to the farms, but there were plenty of small ones, eight and nine and ten years old.

"You kids. You get buckets and fill them at the spring. Or the trough by the school. Haul 'em anywhere anyone needs more water."

Tess was organizing the small, frail, or elderly folks to run a soup kitchen and first aid station. I took a moment to hope we wouldn't need either of them.

When we stepped back outside, we could all see we had our work cut out for us. This wasn't just a lone tree smoldering a bit. This was a nightmare well on its way to reality.

Johnny took a good look at the mass of dark smoke below the town and bellowed more orders.

"Franny! Run to the depot and have old Elliott telegraph to stop the trains!"

The station master was too old, and too twisted up with rheumatism, to do much. But he could stop the trains from running into the fire.

"You, you, and you!" Johnny pointed at three men. "Get those tools we collected from the loggers. In the shed around back."

Franny ran for the station, the three men for the shed, and the rest of us turned to consider the smoke. Only for a moment, until the Ninja Librarian jolted us out of our shock.

"Right, then, we'd best see to those tubs of water." He moved briskly off toward the bathhouse, not running but covering the ground in a hurry anyway. The women and children scattered to their jobs, Rose Herberts directing them here and there, as cool and calm as could be. Johnny and I stood in the street and studied the smoke.

We weren't shocked anymore, but we did need to figure out what to do first.

"Let's run the fire break from the creek out over to where the cliff drops off," I suggested, and Johnny nodded.

"But we should start from right in front of town and work both ways. We've saws and axes, but we'll need picks and shovels—bring whatever you have, men, and let's get it done."

That was when Franny came back, still at a run. "Johnny! Elliott says the line is dead! The fire must've cut it!"

After that, things got busy.

I barely noticed when new folks started arriving to help. Some came with teams and plows to turn up bare dirt that the fire couldn't cross. Hank and Yance came with one horse and their old plow.

"Pa's plowing a ring round our place, just in case. Then he'll be in."

After an hour or two, Johnny took me aside where no one could hear.

"I don't like this, Al."

I didn't either. The plume of smoke was getting bigger.

"We need to tackle the fire itself, not just build a line around the town," I said.

"I believe in this case a line closer to the fire might be wise." We hadn't even noticed when Tom joined us. He was pretty wet, but he had a book in his hand and his confidence seemed to have returned. "This suggests setting a smaller fire in front of the big one, to widen the line. When they meet, the fires appear to diminish each other, if this man writes truly."

We looked at the fire, then at each other.

"Let's give it a try." We rounded up about a third of our crew and left the Ninja Librarian in charge of the town's defenses.

Hauling axes, shovels, plows—and flint and tinder—a dozen or so of us plunged down the slope toward the blaze. From a rock outcrop in a clearing, we finally saw the blaze itself.

Bad enough, but not as bad as I'd imagined. I began to think maybe we had a chance. We studied the land, making our plans. That was when I realized that, in addition to the men we'd brought, we had a crew of boys—including Tommy Colson, but also including my students from Endoline. They must've seen the smoke and arrived in town just in time to follow me.

That was when I got the idea.

Maybe it was because boys like so much to play in the creek and build dams and such. Maybe it was also because the terrain just there sort of suggested it. I handed Johnny my firestarter.

"You take the men and start your fire break."

"What're you up to?"

"The boys and I are going to re-route this here creek, and wet down the backside of your fire," I said.

We worked like the devil himself was scorching us, while the sun rose over the mountain, then while it disappeared behind a new bank of clouds and smoke. We were pretty far along before I realized how dim it had grown again, and peered up through the smoke to see the bottom of a black cloud bulging with rain.

Johnny and his crew had lit their line of brush and grass in front of the main fire, and were mostly just watching it, and beating it back to be sure it didn't become a monster of its own. Johnny glanced at the sky, then came over to see how we did.

Our channel was ready. Hank and Yance were putting the final stones on our diversion dam, and the other boys lengthened the new channel or gathered to start digging through the bank to let the water in. The new stream would run across the meadow before pouring over the rocks and, we hoped, drowning the fire.

At least dampening it. There was less water in the creek than I'd hoped for when I had my idea.

"It'll put out your fire first," I worried to Johnny. Another problem I hadn't foreseen.

"Let it. I think we've done what we can with it."

I turned back to my crew. "Let 'er rip!"

They tore through the last bit of the bank, and water began to flow down the new channel. It wasn't a torrent, because so late in the summer the creek was more of a rivulet. But we had water going where it might help. And we'd backed it up while we built our channel, so there was a good burst at the start.

Just as the water reached the pour-off, the sky opened and it began to rain. A few scattered drops turned in seconds into a downpour so heavy I couldn't see across the meadow to the fire.

We stared a moment, then raced after our flood to check the results.

We had to get pretty close to see much of anything, the downpour was that thick. But already the fire looked less awful. Water hit it from above and below, and in minutes, the new fuel it might have devoured was sodden. So were we, but we didn't mind. We could all see our chance.

"Run to town," I yelled over the storm to Tommy. "Fetch them all. We can stop it right now

143

if we try!"

Two hours later, we knew we'd done it. We were soaking wet, filthy with mud and ash, and beat to the socks. But that fire wasn't going to eat our town, nor anything else.

The only question we had left was if my idea had done any good, or we'd just gotten lucky with the rain.

I could live without an answer to that one.

17 THE NINJA LIBRARIAN SHAKES THINGS UP

I suppose I expected that once we'd put out the fire—or the rain had, to be more honest about it and give credit where it belongs—we'd just go back to doing what we always do, without a thought. And, in a way, we did. All my students came to school, only a little grubby about the hands and fingernails to show what they'd done the day before. That mix of mud and ash stuck hard.

But none of us could settle to our work. It wasn't just that we were still excited by our close call, which had been even closer for some from the farms than it had been for the town. Eunice said their outer field had burned, and it had been only a few weeks until harvest. They would feel the pinch of that. I made a mental note to ask Miss Cornelia to restart the lunch brigade. It might be a hungry winter for some.

All that was disruptive enough, and then Peggy

delivered the final blow to educational order for the day.

"Hey! Did anyone see 'Mayor' Burton yesterday?"

I could hear the sarcasm in the word *mayor*. Peg never did think much of the man, but usually she kept a bit quieter, because we all liked MaryBeth and didn't hold her accountable for her parents.

I glanced at MaryBeth now, sitting very still and a little slumped in her seat. Her face turned red, and then, to my surprise, she squared her shoulders and spoke up.

"He stayed in. Mama climbed up and wet down our roof, but Papa said he'd hurt his back and he didn't do anything!"

I glanced at the hands folded on her desk. Yes, MaryBeth had come out and helped with the digging and hauling. Her nails were ragged, and neither hard scrubbing nor fine soap could clean the last of the dirt from beneath them.

Now everyone looked at her. MaryBeth had never said anything about her father before. She looked scared and defiant and humiliated.

"I hate it!" She burst out. "He calls himself mayor just because he's the richest man in town. But he never *does* anything. All of you have fathers who *do* things!"

Kind-hearted Janey went and hugged her. "Don't be sorry he's rich," she advised, "whatever else you may be mad about. Being rich must be. . . nice."

"But you all hate me for it!" MaryBeth wailed.

"No we don't, you goose." That was Peggy, comforting in her own way. "We know its not your fault. And you're never stuck up." Unlike your parents, Peg managed not to add.

"What we need," Tommy suggested, "is to elect a new mayor."

"Right!" The chorus included everyone present, including me—and MaryBeth.

"That's right," Peggy said. "I've been asking around, and we've never had an election. MaryBeth's right. Her Pa just up and declared himself mayor."

"So how do you have an election?" Joey asked. Everyone turned to look at the teacher.

"I don't know," I said. "But I know where we go to find out."

"The library!" they chorused.

"This whole class is going right over there and learning everything there is to know about elections."

I didn't know what my Primer class, especially the two who had just joined us when school opened a week or so back, could do. I'd think of something. I skipped roll call and the flag salute and we marched right over to the library.

Of course it was hours until the library officially opened, but I didn't let that stop us. I'd have done it just for the look on Tom's face when he realized the whole school was descending on him about ten minutes past sun-up.

The kids left it to me to explain.

"We need to know how to hold an election."

"Any election, or a particular one?"

"An election in this town, because we need a real mayor."

Tom didn't seem surprised. "How was it done in the past?" He addressed the question to all of us, and though several kids shrugged their ignorance, Peggy had more to say.

"That's just it! There's never *been* an election! An' I say it's time we had a real mayor, if we gotta have one at all!"

"I see." He gave it some thought. "If this town has a charter," he began.

Tommy interrupted. "Fat chance!"

Tom went on. "A charter will say how elections are to be conducted. If there is none, then we will need to consider the conventions honored in our fair state and our nation." He looked over the motley collection of students waiting to receive his wisdom, then turned to scan the bookshelves.

In a matter of minutes, he had books in the hands of most of them, and they were eagerly reading how elections have been run from Colonial days to the present, and from one corner of the world to another.

I ended up taking the primer students into the corner and resuming lessons in letters and numbers, until we had something they could handle.

After a time, exclamations began flying, most of them dismayed.

"This says that back when all there were was colonies, only fellows with money got to vote!"

"In this one, you had to have a certain number of acres of land."

Then a truly anguished cry from Peggy. "This says that in the United States, women can't vote and they can't run for office!"

"Well, sure," Tommy said from what he thought was a safe distance. "Everyone knows women can't think." Every girl in the class jumped on him.

Since they knew he was teasing, I didn't have to get mean. If he'd been serious, they might have done some real damage. As it was, a crisp, "Children! Not in the library!" was enough to quell the riot.

When order had restored itself, Peggy said with dignity, "I know everyone here says women can't vote. But I thought that was just them saying it because they didn't want to share. Anyhow, what's the good of an election if half the people can't vote?"

No one had any answers for that.

After an hour or so, I excused myself and went to see Tess. She was only just up, but if my students were going to start a revolution, I wanted her with us.

Within two days the idea had spread all over town. "Mayor" Burton didn't much like it, but he couldn't do anything about it.

The students began planning. I had decided that planning and running an election, and maybe the campaigns too, would be a great lesson. Groups of children got together and started picking their candidates.

Things got interesting when Peggy, Janey, Eunice, and MaryBeth came to me with very solemn faces.

"Teacher, we have to find some way to let women vote."

"*And* to hold office, teacher, because we want to run Mrs. Herberts for mayor."

Well. They just wanted the impossible.

And yet the only people in town who had shown near as much ability as Mrs. Herberts to organize folks were Tess and Johnny. The owner and bartender at Two-Timin' Tess's Tavern wouldn't draw a lot of votes. And Tess was another woman.

"I want Tess," Peggy echoed my thoughts. "But Ma thinks folks wouldn't want to elect a woman who runs a Tavern, not even a nice one like hers."

"She's probably right," I said.

"Of course, Ma doesn't think anyone will elect any woman."

"I hope she doesn't mind when we prove her wrong." I hoped I wasn't just being optimistic. I still didn't even know if we could find a way around the laws. "But one thing I know," I added. "Our first elected woman will have to be darn near perfect."

I knew that was the truth, and it made me cranky. We'd put up with a useless drone like Mr. Burton for years, but folks wouldn't elect a hard-working woman to replace him, unless she was first cousin to the angels.

Peggy skipped right to the important thing. "So how are we gonna get votes for women?"

"They come to me like I know everything!"

Tom corrected my stance and considered me for a moment. "And you come to me expecting that I will have all the answers."

I felt myself turning red. Redder, I should say, because our lessons always leave me sweating and red-faced, even down in the basement of the library where it stays cool. "Who do you go to for all the answers?"

I really wanted to know.

Tom just laughed. "I have a library full of books."

"Fine. Then get them to tell you how to get votes for women."

He ignored my tone, as he usually did when I got grumpy. "I trust you wish to know if we can allow women of this town to vote for our mayor."

"Yeah. And," I took a deep breath and plunged ahead, "to be elected mayor."

I had finally managed to startle Tom, if only for a moment.

"What? A woman can't. . . ." He stopped himself. "I forgot where I am. But of course a woman can, if society will only allow it."

"Women run stuff all the time, and in this town they sure accomplish more than the fellows."

Tom got a distant look in his eyes, as though he were studying bookshelves in his mind. "Keep doing that," he directed me. Then he turned and took the steps to the library two at a time.

I kept doing my drills for another hour and a half, but he never came back.

When I dragged myself up the stairs and peeked into the library, Tom sat as his desk, a dozen books open around him. He waved a dismissing hand at me without looking up.

The Ninja Librarian dropped his bombshell the next afternoon, calling together the children, Tess, Johnny, and anyone else who was interested in the idea of an election.

"Electoral law says that local jurisdictions can establish voter qualifications for local elections, as long as they are no more restrictive than those of the state or territory at large." We all spent a moment translating that, before he went on. "Nowhere in the constitution of our nation or state does it say that women cannot either vote or hold office. As long," he added to me while the others exclaimed over this, "as long as you don't consider the sole use of the masculine pronoun to exclude the feminine. Grammatical rules say that both 'he' and 'man' can refer to both genders."

He got everyone's attention back and added the best part. "In fact, up in Wyoming, women are voting for all but federal offices."

"Well I'll be dipped," Johnny said.

That pretty well summed it up.

"So how do we make our local rules?" asked Tess, who never lost her grip on essentials.

"We establish an elections commission."

"And how do we do that?" Tess sounded a little aggravated.

"My books offer no guidance," Tom admitted.

"Well, then," Peggy said. "I say we just make one. Let's make Mr. Tom, Tess, and Miss Cornelia our whatchamacallit."

"I second that!" Janey hollered.

These kids really had been studying up on how to run a government. I was proud of them, though I might have chosen different commissioners. They hadn't even needed prompting.

"All those in favor?" I called for a vote before anyone could think too much.

A chorus of "Aye!" "Yeah!" "You bet!" and "Me too!" followed. No one voted against.

"Well. That's it, then," said Mrs. Holstead. "You three decide when and how we'll hold the election, and who-all votes. Don't forget to figure out how far out of town we should draw the line on who's part of Skunk Corners."

"And then," Peg announced, "we can elect Mrs. Herberts."

I glanced at Tommy. He shrugged.

"We had our own little election after school. We agreed we should all support one candidate. I wanted Johnny, or Mr. Tom, but the girls outvoted me. That's how democracy works, right?"

Things happened fast after that. Within three days, our electoral commission had declared an election to be held in four weeks. They announced that all persons living within two miles of the Skunk Corners Town Hall could vote, as long as they were at least eighteen. Candidates were to register with them within the week.

We brought Mrs. Herberts in first thing. I'd thought she might be reluctant.

"No, dearie," she said. "I like organizing things. And my shop doesn't keep me so busy these days. If you can get the folk to elect me, I'll be your mayor."

We might have had a fight on our hands if the men had gotten together behind someone like Mr. Johnson, who we all respected. But after ranting and raving and threatening not to run, Mr. Burton had declared himself in. Then he tried to say the election was unlawful. After that, he and his supporters—Mr. Tolliver the banker and a few other men—tried to say that women couldn't vote.

By that time, I could see that even if only the men got to vote, Rose Herberts would beat him like a dusty rug. Her campaign was going strong, but he refused to take it seriously, insisting that everyone knew women couldn't run things, so why worry? To be honest, most people were treating the whole thing as a joke. In a way, they were right. Skunk Corners didn't need a mayor, so what difference did it make? But we'd done our homework. This election would be real.

I suppose it was wrong to use the students to campaign, but they were having so much fun, and learning so much, that I let them.

So my new Primer students learned to spell "Vote for Rose Herberts" by lettering and coloring signs. Then Tommy came up with a slogan that they could use to practice all twenty-six letters: "Rose Herberts acts quickly when making food extra good or voting justice to puny bozos." It wasn't a very good slogan, but it was a good writing exercise.

It rained on election day, so everyone came to the library to vote, though we'd intended to hold it in the town square. The children took turns standing at the door and passing out ballots. They'd spent the previous two days hand-lettering them all. Skunk Corners doesn't have a newspaper anymore, and when the editor fled ten years back, he took his press with him.

Maybe a hundred folks came through and voted. I hadn't known there were so many of us. Some took it real serious, and some made jokes, many on the lines of how we didn't need a mayor anyway, so they were sticking with Mr. Burton, who didn't do anything.

I wasn't sure that made sense.

As for me, I darn near burst with pride and excitement when I dropped my ballot in the box Hank and Yance had made. I might never get to do it again, but at least I'd voted once in my life. Miss Cornelia presided over the box, personally thanking every voter—and making certain they only voted once.

Mrs. Holstead presided over a tea urn, passing out hot drinks to those who were cold and wet, which was most folks.

Mr. Burton came early to vote for himself, then hung around trying to shake hands. Tom reminded him he wasn't allowed to campaign in a polling place, making a vague gesture toward his Ninja mask when he seemed inclined to argue. To my regret, Mr. Burton took himself off home. I'd have enjoyed seeing him kicked into the mud.

Mrs. Herberts voted and then retreated to Tess's, where the girls plied her with tea and scones.

When it got dark, we closed the polls and got down to counting votes. I handed out slates to everyone there, including six or seven of my students, who never seemed to go home for chores, and Mr. Johnson of the Mercantile, Mr. Holstead, and Eunice's mother, who just refused to go home until she knew who won.

Then Tom pulled out the ballots one by one and read off the vote, holding it up so we could all see he did it accurately. In the end, our ten tally-keepers had eight different numbers marked down. But it didn't matter, because they all said the same thing.

Rose Herberts was our new mayor by a vote of roughly three to one.

I didn't know what they'd have thought about our election back there in Washington D.C., where they say women can't do things. I didn't care.

In Skunk Corners, women can do pretty much anything we set our minds to.

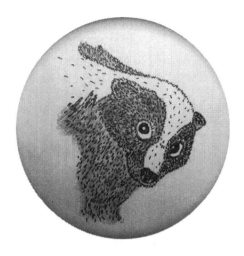

18 THE NINJA LIBRARIAN BLOWS UP AGAIN

I'd like to say that things in Skunk Corners changed fast with our new mayor in charge. I'd like to, but I'd be lying.

Actually, for the first several weeks, Mrs. Herberts spent all her spare time at the library, studying up on what mayors do.

"I'm not rushing into anything," she said whenever anyone asked about her plans for the town. "We've gone a long time with no town government. It won't hurt us to wait a mite longer so's we can do it right."

That convinced just about everyone that she was awfully smart and would do the town proud. The ones who still thought a woman couldn't be mayor said it just showed she didn't know what she was doing. They conveniently forgot that Mr. Burton hadn't ever done anything, including educate himself about town government.

We were getting well on toward winter when Mayor Herberts began to take hold. On a cold November day she called a Town Meeting. Everyone crowded into Tess's barroom, which is a little bigger than the library, to hear what the mayor had to say.

With so many people in the room, the ones near the stove had to strip to shirtsleeves in the heat, while those near the door pulled coats and scarves tight against the cold wind that found its way past the boards that had shrunk over the summer. Once folks settled, Mayor Herberts stood up.

"Since you're all here, I thought about giving you all the speech I never got to make back on the Fourth," she began. "But I'll spare you that. I want to say I see three things our town needs."

She held up one finger. "First, a proper School Board and proper funds for the school. Miss Alice does a fine job," she said.

I blushed, too abashed to even care she'd called me "Miss Alice."

"Let's show we care by giving her a decent wage and enough books for her students."

"An' a stove that works!" I couldn't see him, but I recognized Tommy's voice.

Mayor Herberts held up a second finger, with just a nod and a smile for the interruption. "Second, we need some law enforcement. At least some rules. We don't need a Sheriff, but we need to know that fights will stay out of the street and won't include guns!"

No one could argue with that without looking as though they liked fighting, so folks stayed quiet. She held up a third finger.

"Finally, we need a plan. Instead of leaving it to our children to come up with things that will make all our lives better, things like our windmill, let's think about what we need. And let's plan for trouble, too, so we know who's in charge next time there's a fire or a storm."

"Why?" Someone hollered from the back of the crowd. "We done just fine!" A chorus of mostly male voices sounded in agreement.

"You think so, Mr. Colson?" It was Miss Cornelia, not Mayor Herberts, who answered. "How long did it take for someone to come make sure you all were safe after that storm? And how long would some of us right here in town have waited for help if Big Al here hadn't started folks moving? I say Rose is right, and I'll back you all the way, dearie!"

I smothered a laugh. She was so excited, and the menfolk so kerflummoxed, being mostly raised to be polite to old ladies. They couldn't argue without being rude. Maybe it was taking advantage to use that, but men had taken advantage for so long that I couldn't feel bad.

I stood behind the bar with Tom and watched while Mayor Herberts got the crowd to elect a Town Council and a School Board to make her ideas come true.

I wasn't surprised when they put Tom on the School Board. Everyone knew he had more education than the rest of us put together. It was more unexpected when someone nominated Hilda, and she, too, was voted in.

Ike Holstead was the third board member, and I felt pretty good about maybe having some help, or at least some sympathy, at last.

The Council included Mr. Johnson, Mr. Tolliver—we didn't much like him, but he did know business—and Eunice's ma, Prudence Reeves. Politics seemed to have taken a hold on her, and she'd jumped right up to volunteer.

Of course, for all that, not much changed in

Skunk Corners. Tom brought the School Board to class a few days after the meeting. They not only watched me teach, which made me right uncomfortable, but they took inventory of all the repairs our school needed. That gave me some hope. More pay would be nice, but I would settle for better chinking in the logs and a door that closed properly. And that new stove.

Two days after that, I found Tom studying a book on boilers and steam heaters. To my horror, he already had most of my boys involved. This time, Peggy kept her distance. She was too busy studying her Advanced Algebra book so she could teach it to Tommy and me. We worked on it during morning break. Fifteen minutes wasn't much time, but it was about as much as we two could swallow.

But that girl gave a lot of homework.

After a few days of watching materials accumulate behind the school once more, I confronted the Ninja Librarian.

"What on earth are you doing? I thought we'd settled this boiler nonsense once and for all!"

"There is no reason for concern, Alice. I am considering the plan very carefully and will personally supervise the design and construction."

I remembered how he'd admitted last winter that he didn't know much about steam engines.

"Hmph." My grumpy-old-lady imitation had worked well on Bill Jenkins, but the Ninja Librarian was made of sterner stuff.

Much sterner.

"I assure you, Alice, there will be no explosion this time."

Like a fool, I believed him.

Soon enough, I was caught up in the plan despite my distrust of all things related to steam and boilers. That sprang from the attempt the previous winter to build a pump and boiler that would provide hot water to school and library alike. The explosion that ended that experiment had blown out all my windows, and it was only luck it hadn't blown Crazy Jake and Wild Harry Colson sky high, or killed half my pupils.

"We are utilizing a much simpler and superior design in this instance," Tom assured me. "We do not have to pump the water, as the windmill has solved that issue efficiently. I just wish to heat it and pipe it into my kitchen." He got a very wistful look, maybe the most revealing expression I'd ever seen on his usually inscrutable face.

"I miss very few aspects of city life, Alice, but a hot bath in winter must be counted among them."

Well! He'd finally told me something of himself, whether he'd meant to or not.

"The city?" I asked, as innocent as a new-born chipmunk. "You came here from some city?"

"Yes," he said. Only that, and nothing more, as Mr. Poe says in that poem in McGuffey's Sixth reader. It made for a good poem, but it's frustrating in real life.

Tom's face was solemn, but there was a gleam in his eye that I'd learned meant he enjoyed tormenting me. But I had figured something out.

"You never lived in the sticks before!"

He inclined his head. "I concede the point."

"And you could have gone back—you *did* go back. But," the wonder of it struck me. "You came back to us. Even without hot baths."

"I did."

For one moment I wondered what he'd given up besides baths to come here. And why on earth he thought Skunk Corners was worth it.

Of course, Skunk Corners is a pretty nice place compared to Endoline, or even Two-Bit and Pine Knot, especially since Tom straightened out the rowdies and reopened the library. But it wasn't heaven. Was every place out there just as bad? Maybe so. Though, I'd been to Lupine and it wasn't so bad. Surely a city would be even nicer than Lupine.

Made me think, he did. I'd always figured just about anywhere would be an improvement on our piece of Skunk Mountain. Maybe I was wrong.

I was so caught up in this new idea that I forgot to pursue the question of explosions, which was no doubt Tom's intention. He'd found a way to keep me from trying to stop his project, and he knew it. Every time I started to ask too many questions, or to protest the likely disaster in the making, he'd pass me some tidbit about his past life.

In that way I learned he'd gotten his education from something called Aberystwyth University, that he had no family, and that he was not the only Ninja Librarian out there.

I'm not sure he meant to tell me that last. It happened like this. When I saw the nearly-finished boiler, out behind the bathhouse, of course, but still too close for comfort, I blew my top.

"You boys are all crazy as songbirds in springtime! That thing looks just like the last one, and you are *not* going to fire it up!"

"Yes, we are!" Tommy shot back. "And it'll work, too, because we did it right this time!"

"No you ain't!" I was mad enough to leave grammar by the wayside and answer him in his own language.

That was when I heard Tom mutter, "I bet none of the other Ninjas have to deal with this."

I think I'm getting smarter, because I didn't follow up on the comment right then. I just stowed it away in my head to think about later. Besides, I was busy.

In the end, I lost the argument, as I might have expected. You can't talk sense to a herd of males.

Three days later, I caught Tommy, Joey, and even Petey Rossiter, Peggy's brother, hauling buckets of coal to the bathhouse. I followed them and found a large pile of all kinds of fuel next to a shining—and undeniably solid-looking—boiler. A boiler which might even have been meant for the job from the start, and a brick fire-box. Hank and Yance were putting the finishing touches on the brickwork, so at least they'd gotten something practical out of this.

I had to look twice. Those were *decorative* touches the boys were adding. Was that my boys making something pretty for the sake of being pretty?

Tom puttered about the boiler, polishing the reservoir—a waste of effort in my mind, since the first fire would discolor it for good. But since he was also carefully checking all the joints and welds, I didn't say anything.

I stood there with my hands on my hips, torn between my distrust of all things steam-powered—and my desire for a hot bath. With the coming of Fall I'd gone back to sponge baths in my zinc washtub, but I can't say I was happy about it. There wasn't enough sun to warm the basalt—or the water pipes atop it.

I wanted a hot, neck-deep bath in a warm room.

It's just that I wanted to avoid explosions even more.

"Please do not worry yourself, Alice," Tom said, reading my mind as usual. "As you can see, I have ensured a solid boiler."

"*And* we got a safety-valve this time." Hank

pointed to an odd object atop the boiler.

Recognizing defeat when I met it, and hoping for a hot bath, I asked, "When do you test it?"

I intended to be just close enough to see what happened. And far enough off to be out of range of flying bricks and hot steel.

"Tomorrow after school we should put on the final touches," Tom said. "We'll fire it up Saturday morning and have a good breakfast at the library while it heats. I believe I have finally perfected my sourdough, er, flapjacks." The local name didn't come smoothly to his lips.

I hadn't known he was studying to cook, either. Seemed like there was an awful lot going on I didn't know about.

As planned, two days later I came out of the school as the lot of them trooped to the bathhouse. I stayed well back and watched while they lit the fire and stoked it to a good roar. We all watched for a few minutes, Tom checking the pipe joints for leaks and drips.

"Everything appears to be sound," he announced at last. "Let us repair to the library and breakfast while the water heats."

From Tom's apartment in the rear of the library, the bathhouse was out of sight. Every few minutes one of the boys would go peer out the one library window that offered a view that direction. After a half hour, Hank and Yance went to stoke the fire.

A few minutes later, Tommy went to check progress, and we heard his voice from the other room. "Uh-oh."

As we all dashed out to see what worried Tommy, I heard the Ninja Librarian mutter, "I am *certain* the other Librarians don't have these problems."

He spoke as though to himself. Yet I was sure

he knew I'd hear.

Any thoughts of Tom's mysterious past were blown from my head when I looked out the window.

The entire heat-pressurized contents of the boiler spewed geyser-like from the safety valve.

"By Jove," I managed between whoops of laughter, "I believe you've invented a hot shower!"

Tom laughed, though I thought he had to force it some. He'd been that set on a bath. "I wish to point out, Alice, that nothing has exploded."

That was true enough, but in a minute the shower of water, however hot, had quenched the fire, and the spray died as the pressure in the tank dropped.

"See?" Tommy said. "A shower that shuts itself off."

"Alas," Tom said, "as one must stand in the fire to enjoy the shower, I fear the appeal is limited."

Smelling burnt flapjacks, he turned and raced back to his kitchen, leaving the rest of us to contemplate the now-sodden device behind the bathhouse.

"Don't worry, Teacher," Hank said.

"Right." Yance added. "I know just what we need to do."

I looked at the twins, and they looked at the boiler.

I hoped they were right. I surely did.

19 THE NINJA LIBRARIAN BEATS A BLIZZARD

I was neck deep in a tub of hot water when the blizzard hit.

To my delight, a delight almost as great as that of the Ninja Librarian, Hank and Yance had been correct. They'd easily fixed the boiler system so it worked. Now Tom and I could enjoy arguing over whose turn it was for a bath, since it took a couple of hours to heat a tubful of water.

I heard the wind first, coming down the mountain with a roar like a runaway train. When it hit, a blast of icy air blew through the cracks between the boards of the bathhouse. Until that moment, I'd have said there weren't any gaps, but the chill drafts drove me from the tub and back into my winter woolies.

I rubbed my short hair as dry as I could before

opening the door and venturing out. Even so, by the time I'd run the dozen or so yards to my own door ice had begun to form on the wet ends. The first snow hit as I slammed the door behind me. They weren't the lovely soft snow flakes that the poets in the children's Readers like to prattle on about. It was a shower of icy needles hard and sharp enough to flay the skin from your face.

I grabbed the heavy coat I hadn't worn to the bathhouse and pulled it on, shivering.

It had been a brisk, but not cold, December afternoon when I'd gone out to stoke the bathhouse fire.

It had been a cold, but not icy, evening when I'd gone for my bath in the water heated by Tom's ingenious boiler.

Now the mercury was racing to the bottom of the thermometer as though it hunted a place to hide from the storm. My little room was as cold as ex-mayor Burton's heart. I set about building up the fire that had died back to coals while I was in the bath.

Thank heavens the children would all be safely home long since, even those who had gone to the library after school. I wondered what Tom thought of this weather. We'd had no such storms last winter, and being from some city I supposed he'd not know about storms. Did they even have weather in cities?

I could find that out later. A body couldn't go visiting in this.

There should have been some light left outside, but the storm had ended the day with a firm, dark hand. I lit my lamp and watched the flame dance in the drafts the wind drove through my room.

Sighing, I stuffed rags in all the cracks around the door and windows. I piled all my blankets on my bed, took off my boots and dungarees, and put on a second pair of long underwear. Then I set the lamp by the bed and crawled under the covers with my new book.

It was the best of times, it was the worst of times. I shivered, and put Mr. Dickens aside in favor of *Robinson Crusoe.* A south-sea island seemed a better choice on this night.

I read until I reached the place where Crusoe finds a footprint in the sand and realizes for the first time that he's not alone on the island. It must've made Crusoe sweat some, but it made me shiver. Though that might've been because my stove needed stoking again. The School Board hadn't managed all those repairs they'd decided were necessary, and the wind sucked the heat out of my room as fast as the stove could put it in.

Just as I was about to get up and see to the fire, my door crashed open, pushed by the wind, and Hank and Yance blew in. They wrestled the door shut behind them before looking around. They dripped on my floor as the snow began to melt off them. Then, seeing that I was abed, they turned matching shades of red and began backing toward the door.

"Oh, for Pete's sake!" I reached for my pants. "Turn around, then, and I'll get up."

Once I was decently clad—though I'd been wearing two pair of long underwear and my duffle coat before, so I'm not sure what was so indecent— I made them sit down by the stove and thaw.

"Why are you here?" I demanded. "You should've been home long since."

They shook their heads. "We was workin' on some cabinets with Mr. Holstead. When the storm started, we high-tailed it for home, but we wasn't far along when we knowed we'd not make it." That was probably the longest speech I'd ever heard Hank make.

"So we headed back to town, thinkin' we'd go to the library," Yance said.

"So why in tarnation are you here? Not that I mind," I hastened to add, before they could start edging toward the door again.

"Got blowed off course."

"*Blown*, Yance, not blowed."

"Either way, we lit up here, and we figured we'd better stop. Seemed if we didn't grab the first shelter we came to, we might end up somewhere out in the woods and you'd find us in the spring."

He was right about that. They were also cold and wet, so I set about making them warm and dry.

I started a pot of stew, as well, though I'd no meat for it. It'd be hot, at least.

We had just filled our bowls when the door banged open again. This time it was Crazy Jake and Wild Harry, and between them, the Ninja Librarian, well-bundled but still about half their size.

"We was all over at Tess's when the storm hit," Jake said. "But he—" He jerked his head at Tom— "He said he had to see you. Since he wouldn't hear sense and stay put, me an' Harry thought we'd best make sure he didn't blow away."

"I assure you I am not mad," Tom said, removing his outer layer and shaking the snow from it. "But we do have a situation which requires some thought."

I glanced at the boys. Hank and Yance never did manage to finish school, though their success at carpentry said they weren't all dumb. Neither are Jake and Harry, sometimes. But I wasn't looking at the best thinkers in Skunk Corners, either. Tom understood my glance.

"I believe we may also have need of some muscle before we're done, so perhaps it is as well to have the young men here."

I didn't like the sound of that, and not just because the boys were smart enough to figure out what we were thinking about their brains.

I was all for spending the night thinking by the stove. But muscle implied going outside, and we'd be crazy to do that. Tom just didn't understand these storms. We could fix that.

Tom pulled off his boots, copying the boys, and sat on one of the chairs Hank had run to bring from the school room. We all put our feet under the stove.

I noticed that Tom had hung his coat on the chair and put his boots near to warm and dry—the acts of a man who expects to need them again.

I definitely did not like the direction this was taking.

I tried to console myself. If he'd meant to go back out, he'd not have taken his things off in the first place.

I didn't believe that, but I pretended to.

"The thing is," Tom said, "that I am concerned about your friend Wes."

I felt a moment of fear and squelched it.

"Why? He's lived on this mountain longer'n any of us. You know he's been through heaps of storms."

"That is true, Alice. But," he looked at me and there was no glimmer of humor on his face. "Wes is not only older now, but I fear he may put himself in the way of danger."

That made some sense. What was different about this storm, for Wes, was that Bill Jenkins was on the mountain too. But that couldn't be all.

"If you're thinking of Bill Jenkins," I argued, "he was up there all last winter and did just fine."

"That is true," Tom said. "But one thing has changed."

Finally I saw it.

"Billy! It's Friday. He came for Billy this afternoon?"

Tom nodded.

"And you're afraid they might not have made it back to the claim in time." I was already reaching for my own boots when Tom spoke.

"I do not see how they could have done so."

"But you say you are worried about Wes, not Billy," I pointed out, stopping with my boots in my hand.

"That is correct."

I put my boots back down. "Why?"

Jake put me out of my misery. "Because Bill and Billy made it back to the Tavern not long after the storm started. Jenkins saw the weather coming in and turned back."

"But Wes won't know that," I realized.

"That is the substance of my concern, yes," Tom said. "I fear he will worry about them and venture in search."

I cocked an ear to listen to the howling winds. "He'll not go out tonight. He's been here too long. He knows."

Knows, I didn't say, that anyone caught out on a night like this stood no chance, save by the most extraordinary woodsman's know-how and a lot of luck.

"I believe you are correct," Tom said.

I relaxed. "Then we needn't worry."

"We need not worry until the storm abates," he said. "I believe that as soon as the wind lessens, Wes will venture in search of them. I do not believe he will be safe."

I eyed the Ninja Librarian. "You seem to know an awful lot about him."

"We have conversed." He shrugged that off. "I also know something of storms of this ilk."

"But you're from the city!"

"Weather strikes the city as well as the woods, Alice. As it happens, the city of my youth was subject to storms much worse than this."

Storms worse than this? I had thought cities were places apart from all natural forces. Now he was telling me the weather could be worse in some far-off city than in Skunk Corners?

Once again, I was forced to wonder if Skunk Corners was so bad, or if every place had problems. But I couldn't stop for long to think about it, because I did know one thing. The Ninja Librarian was right about Wes. If he was worried about Billy, he wouldn't hesitate to risk himself if there was any chance at all of living through it.

I had been studying with Wes for several months now. I had great faith in his knowledge and self-reliance. But could anyone handle weather like this, let alone an old man?

Could we?

"I believe," Tom said, "that we should prepare ourselves for an expedition, then await a break in the storm."

"Not you," Harry protested. "Yer too—" He stopped and I knew he'd almost said "old." "Yer too little," he finished, instead.

Tom looked at us. It was true that he was an inch shorter and unknown pounds lighter than the smallest of us. But I didn't think that would stop him, and I for one wouldn't try.

"None of us has dependents," Tom said, as though Hank hadn't spoken. "We'll all six go, unless someone wishes to be let off."

"Let's get what we need," Yance said by way of answering for us all.

I considered the twins. I thought of them as boys, but they were seventeen and full-grown. They had the right to take their own risks, I guessed.

"How can we get anything?" Hank asked. "We can't even leave here!"

Well, we rummaged through my supplies for anything that might help, then set my lantern in the window and headed for Tess's. We could see her lantern before we lost sight of mine, so that was okay, though the storm tried to blow us to bits.

Tess gave us the rest of what we needed—ropes and blankets and food and clothes.

"Bring him back here if you can."

We promised, then settled in to doze by the stove in the barroom. Johnny promised to wake us if the storm slackened. He wanted to join the expedition, but Tom wouldn't let him.

"Tess and the girls depend on you." It was the second time he'd shown he figured we could die doing this. I wanted to insist that he stay behind.

I knew better than to suggest it.

It wasn't really dawn when Johnny woke us, but there was a vague lightening of the darkness that must've meant there was a dawn somewhere. The storm had slackened enough to allow us to speak without shouting.

It was as good as we'd get.

Bundled to the eyebrows and lugging our ropes, food, and other gear, we started up the ridge. The snow blasting the exposed skin around my eyes didn't hurt so bad now. A faint light in the sky let us make out the trees well enough that we didn't walk into them, except Harry, once.

The Ninja Librarian wanted to lead, but it took only a minute to show we'd have to take turns. Plowing through calf-deep snow, with the wind in your face, wore a body out fast. As the smallest, Tom had the hardest time. Ninja skills didn't seem to compensate for a lack of bulk in this case.

The trouble was, once we'd passed the

windmill, only Tom and I knew where to go. I took my place in the lead and headed off, lining up in the right direction from the windmill. When I tired and dropped back, I could no longer see the windmill, nor much of anything else. Tom seemed confident, and when he tired, he guided each of the others from behind.

When I moved to the head of the line again, we had about as much daylight as we were going to get. You could see the trees a ways ahead.

Trouble was, I didn't see anything I recognized, and I didn't know if we were still moving in the right direction, other than uphill.

Tom moved up beside me when I stopped. He raised an eyebrow, and I kept my voice low. "Where the blazes are we?"

"I had hoped you would know. I *believe* we are on the ridge just below Mr. Wes's cave." Tom glanced around as though he thought he'd see a sign or something.

I hear in those cities he comes from, everything is marked so you know where you are. Not out here. One tree looks an awful lot like another, especially in a blizzard.

By now the others had come up around us. They might not be the best scholars in my school, but they didn't need a teacher to tell them we were lost.

"Uh-oh," I heard Harry say.

We spent the next two hours trying to figure out where the dickens we were, and where we needed to go search.

When the wind began to pick up again, Tom called us together.

"The storm is returning. I believe we shall have to go home. I am sorry."

I was a great deal sorrier, because when I looked

around, I realized that we'd left a mess of tracks—
and most had filled in or blown away.

Our argument over the way home continued
while the storm grew stronger. Jake put an end to
it.

"Too late!" He shouted over the storm. "We
have to find shelter now!"

The truth of his words struck us, the more as at
that moment the wind knocked Ninja Tom from his
feet.

"There's a bit of a rock overhang yonder," Yance
shouted. "Let's go!"

We followed the twins, and the force of the
wind eased when we reached the outcrop.
Huddling against the lee side of the rocks, we used
the gear we'd hauled to create more shelter. It
wasn't much, but anything was more shelter than
we'd had.

We hadn't a hope of lighting a fire, but Jake and
Harry undertook to try anyway. They'd nothing
better to do.

To my amazement, the boys got a flame. A shot
of coal oil from the lantern we'd carried help get it
going, and a downed tree broken over the rocks
provided fuel. The snow was dry enough to knock
loose from the wood easily, though the cold fuel
burned poorly.

We must've been there a few hours before the
wind dropped some, and the snowfall thinned.
Things were looking better and worse. Better,
because we had a fire and a small pot of soup
going. Worse, because all our tracks had vanished,
and visibility was still lousy. We'd have to wait
out the storm and hope that it would clear enough
before dark that we could see to locate ourselves.

That was when Wes walked around a corner of
the rocks, balanced comfortably atop the snow on a
pair of hand-made snowshoes.

"Good afternoon, gentlemen. Miss Alice."

"Wes!" I climbed to my feet and led him to our fire, as though we were rescuing him rather than the other way around.

"Do I take it you're also searching for Mr. Jenkins and Billy? I grew worried when the storm hit before they could have reached their cabin. I fear I have been unable to find them."

Feeling foolish as a flatfish, I said, "Um, actually we, well, uh."

The Ninja Librarian rescued me. "We thought we ought to find you, to tell you to call off your search. They are safe at Tess's, having wisely turned back at the first signs of the storm."

"Ah." Wes looked us over. Whatever he thought, he didn't say it.

"Lunchtime, what? Mind if I sit in?" He pulled a battered tin mug from a pocket, dipped it full of soup, and sipped cautiously. "Remind me to show you some of the more useful cooking herbs, Alice."

I thought our soup tasted just fine, but perhaps that was due to hours of thrashing about in the snow. I decided not to take offense. Besides, I hadn't made the soup. Jake had.

When we all finished eating, Wes put up his mug and said, "I think I'll go on back to town with you. I would like a word with Mr. Jenkins." He looked around. "I see you haven't snowshoes, so I will go ahead and break trail for you."

We packed up, no one saying much, especially about not knowing which way to go. We just let Wes lead off down the hill and wondered why we hadn't thought of snowshoes.

In a short time, embarrassingly short, we could see the town, as the storm blew itself away.

I dropped back beside the Ninja Librarian, who looked more beat than a Ninja should.

"Do you s'pose he knows?"

Tom looked at me and raised an eyebrow.

Yup. Wes knew. Tom changed the subject. "I believe you doubted we could find him, Alice. Does this adequately satisfy you on that point?"

Seemed to me Wes'd found us. I looked at my teacher and decided not to say so. He wasn't so tired he couldn't make me do my usual evening practice drills, if I were so foolish as to vex him.

"I believe I shall claim the first bath," he said, and dared me to argue.

I didn't. My bed was calling, and I meant to answer.

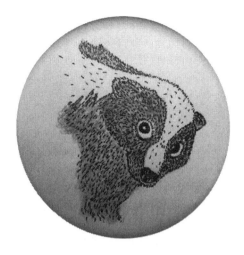

20 THE NINJA LIBRARIAN AND THE TROUBLE IN ENDOLINE

Why is it that every time I think we have Skunk Corners running as smooth as cream on pie, something else goes wrong? It's enough to make me think the world just won't go smoothly. Or won't stay that way.

We'd survived the big blizzard, and the winter hadn't been too bad since. Hot baths helped, though both the Ninja Librarian and I wished we'd built the bathhouse a bit closer to home. That dash through the cold after a bath could freeze you for real.

The school house was finally mostly weather-tight, though my raise hadn't appeared, nor yet the new stove.

My students were making good progress, even Hank and Yance. Those two had learned more since they quit school than in the two years previous. I puzzled over that, seeing as I was the teacher both ways.

All these things were knocked from my head when Ryan showed up for his weekly visit on a gloomy January afternoon. Gloomy described the weather, and gloomy covered his mood, too.

"No, the kids are great, Teacher," he said in response to my questions. I'd tried to get him to call me Al, now we were colleagues, as it were. But he said I was still his teacher, and he didn't want me to forget it. That boy was serious about education and had almost caught up with my Sixth-Reader students in math. His reading was as good as anyone, if he could find things to read.

Endoline had no library, but I happened to know that Tom had long since given Ryan a library card, even if he didn't live in Skunk Corners. I think he made a new rule about all students of the Skunk Corners school being eligible for a card, no matter where they lived. He didn't ever ask me if Ryan was enrolled in the school, which of course he wasn't. Tom must've figured Ryan for my student, and I guess he was right.

Anyway, for a teacher whose students were doing great, Ryan was awfully glum.

"It's not the kids, it's the parents. They say they don't want their kids wasting time in school."

There we were again. The Endoline attitude that made the place such a gawdawful mess.

"Tell them the law says kids have to go until they're fourteen."

"It does?" Ryan studied my face in the lamplight, trying to see if I was funning him. Nobody up on this mountain went to school all the time until they were fourteen. I had every intention of changing that for my students, but Endoline, Two-Bit and Pine Knot only even had schools from time to time.

"Honor bright. Mr. Tom says so."

For a moment, Ryan brightened, then his smile fled. His next words chased mine off, too.

"It's not going to work, Teacher. Mort Black is telling them to keep their kids away from me. He says school made Franny run away, even though she ran before she ever even went to school. And he says he's gonna lock Benny in the woodshed rather'n let him come." He paused, then went on, "But you know what? It's not about kids learning. Black works for whoever owns the lumber mill and the rest of the town, and he just wants to be sure he has lots of people—lots of slaves!—to work for him."

"I don't get it. He can't be wanting little kids."

"Oh, he'll take them from maybe eight or ten. Has 'em run errands and all that. Worst is, folks need the work. The mill mostly owns everything, and they've lost their land, or the trees off it. There's nothin' left up there, Teacher."

I nodded. That sounded like Black. And maybe like big outsiders, too, though I knew little about such critters. I did know that Endoline was dirt poor and getting poorer.

I had another thought.

"Girls too? He has girls working the mill?" Not that girls aren't just as good as boys, mind. I'll argue that any time you like, and knock it into folks' heads if they won't believe me. But most places won't hire them for boys' work.

"Well, the little ones run errands, just like the boys. He puts the older girls to work in the cook house, or doing laundry. Some he hires at the saloon." We both thought about where that could lead. Would even Endoline parents really want that?

"But he pays them all, right?"

"Oh, sure. But hardly nothing, just a, just, just as close to nothin' as you can get!" He was so upset he stuttered over his response.

I could see it. Black would like that. He liked being the boss, and he liked taking advantage. He was mean clean through. And he'd not want a school, because a kid who started learning things might not want to work all his life in a lumber mill. Or her life in a laundry. Those "ideas" he worried school would give them might lead them away from his trap. Besides, he wouldn't like having folks around with more learning than he had, and he didn't have much.

When Black tried to steal our woods, was he aiming to make Skunk Corners another town he could use to serve his, his *masters*? I almost smiled. Mort Black had given himself control by becoming a pawn for someone else. Typical shoddy reasoning. The man could use an education.

"Well, we won't let him get away with it," I declared. "Folks need to be able to make their own choices."

"But how're we gonna stop him? He's mean."

Poison mean. I knew that.

We took the problem to the Ninja Librarian. Tom has always met my most insurmountable problems with a smile that says he sees the ever-so-obvious solution that I've missed. Sometimes it makes me want to hit him, though I'm not dumb enough to try. This time, when I really would have liked to see that look, it wasn't there.

"I do not have an immediate solution to your problem," he began. Ryan looked so crestfallen Tom hastened to add, "I expect, however, that we will think of something. In the meantime, I believe you both have lessons to complete."

At least that sounded more like the annoying librarian we'd come to know and love. I spent the next fifteen minutes explaining out some geometry problems to Ryan, and the hour after that, going through my exercises while answering his questions. Tom insisted I visualize the math and answer Ryan's questions without stopping what I was doing or looking at his work.

Twice I fell over because I couldn't maintain a complex form while explaining an equally complex postulate.

By the time we finished, I was ready for bed. It was late, and the night was cold, but there was a moon and Ryan insisted he needed to go home.

"Pa's away, and I don't like leaving Ma all alone."

Thinking of life in Endoline, I couldn't blame him. "Watch out for lions and skunks, then." I heard a sound, much like a stifled laugh, from the Ninja Librarian, but when I looked at him he was absorbed in his book.

"We'll think of something, Ryan," I said, wanting to encourage him.

He hesitated in the doorway, not looking at all encouraged. "Melville's and Buddy's sisters already stopped coming. Their Pas threatened to lick 'em if they got uppity." Then he stepped into the night and closed the door.

The next day after school, I went to see Franny. Tess had taken over teaching the girl her letters and numbers, with help from Billy. He was now plowing through the Second Reader, several chapters ahead of her. The girl didn't like to come to school and let everyone see her ignorance, so I hadn't seen as much of Franny as I might. But she was needing a little help with her math, so I had said I'd come along.

Tess called Billy to her. "Teacher's come to help Franny with those math problems. You show her up and then go fill the kindling box."

"I really tried, Teacher," said Billy, who took his teaching very seriously indeed. "But you know I'm not so far along with math." He left me at Franny's door and went to do his chores.

Franny showed me into her room, and if she needed help with math, she also suspected that wasn't all of why I'd come. Tess knows the multiplication tables as well as me, and I'd bet she's as good a teacher as I am. She had some other reason she wanted me to see the girl. Still, I insisted on seeing and straightening out the troublesome equations before I sat back and looked at Franny.

I no longer saw the frightened but defiant ragamuffin I'd first met. Julia and Hildy had made her some decent clothes, and she looked like a young woman. It suddenly struck me that she was only a little younger than I. And she was from Endoline.

Where girls had almost no choices.

"Who is Coot Mulligan?" I asked.

Franny looked at her hands, clenched in her lap, and blushed. Then she looked up. "He's just what he sounds like. An old coot who lives even farther up the mountain. But Pa said I could marry him, or I could go to work in the saloon soon's I turned fifteen. I didn't want to do either, so I run off."

"I thought you just came here for school, and I talked you into staying."

"I never had no intention of goin' back. I wanted to come here because of you. Because you got out of Endoline, so I knew it could happen. An' maybe you'd help me. Which you did."

"You knew me? Ryan said none of the kids would remember me."

She rolled her eyes. "I'm as old as he is. Course I remembered you. *You* got away," she said again.

"So did you," I said after a moment. "You've

got just as much nerve as I do."

We thought about that for a while before I said, "Black's got to be stopped. He's trying to shut down Ryan's school. Then they'll be back to having no choices."

She nodded. "I don't know what hold he's got on folks up there, because you'd think the menfolk'd get tired of his ways, even if the women are too beat down to care anymore. But no one does nothin'. I suppose they're all just too desperate."

"He spent the summer trying to make trouble down here," I said.

"That was about you. An' maybe me."

I had no answer to that.

"He's the sort to hate the ones who got away, almost as much as he despises the ones who can't." Neither of us had heard Tess return. "I do believe you hurt his poor little pride."

Her tone made us laugh, but I decided Tess was right. She's almost as good as Tom at seeing what makes people tick.

"So, shutting Ryan down, is that to get at me? Or to keep his hold on folks up there?"

"Or to prove it," Franny suggested.

"Maybe a bit of each," Tess said. "Educated folks are a lot harder to control. And you know that someone like Ryan, now he's learning more, isn't going to stay in Endoline and work in that lumber mill for a pittance. And for some reason Black really does seem to hate you, Al."

I ignored the searching look she gave me. "We have to stop him."

We all agreed about that. We just couldn't figure out how.

Every few days Ryan came down from Endoline, and his face grew longer each time. It got next to impossible to cheer him up. When he told me his school was down to him and Buddy, I wanted to cry. We couldn't lose! But I still had no ideas, and apparently, neither did the Ninja Librarian.

We had nearly despaired when Ryan found us the key. Tom fitted it in the lock, as it were, and we had us a plan.

"Black's been super cranky lately," Ryan reported. "Seems he's got a bad tooth. An' no dentist in Endoline, so he just cusses and knocks folks about."

"Maybe he'll die of it," I muttered.

"Now, Alice," Tom reproved. "That is not a charitable wish."

Before I could point out that I saw no reason for any charity pointed at Mort Black, the Ninja Librarian went on.

"No, every man should have his chance. He needs a dentist and we shall provide him with one." I looked sharp at him, and maybe he wasn't being so charitable after all.

He sent Peggy and Tommy for Tess, and for Enoch Johnson from the Mercantile. Then Tom set Ryan and me to doing forms until they arrived. He'd recently started Ryan on Ninja lessons, too, saying a boy like him in a place like Endoline needed any edge he could get. I think he feared Mort Black might attack him some night.

Only when the others were there did Tom let us stop and lay out his plan. As he did, our grins got bigger. This might actually work.

When Tom finished, Mr. Johnson nodded. "Of course. I still have my tools."

Tess said, "He might recognize me. But I believe Hildy would do the job with pleasure."

"I can't tell him myself," Ryan added. "He hates me. But I'll see to it word gets to him. Then it's up to you." He snickered a bit.

We set to work, and by the next afternoon we had everything ready before Buddy arrived at my door, breathless, with word that Mort Black was on his way.

"He's proddy as a bear in the Spring, an' his face is swole up somethin' turrible," he added. "I reckon he's ready."

He raced off to tell Tom, and I headed for Tess's. When Black rode into town—we could hear him a half mile off, cussing as the jolting of riding even at an easy walk hurt his face—Hildy was dressed in the outfit she and the girls had cobbled together overnight. I helped her gather the evil-looking collection of vials and brews we'd concocted, and we took it all to the Mercantile.

A new sign out front advertised barbering and dentistry within, and I had time to see that Mr. Johnson really did have a barber's chair, as well as a terrifying collection of dental tools. Some looked rather large, and seeing my gaze, he winked.

"I used to treat hosses, too."

I joined Tom, Buddy, Hank, and Yance in the back room, out of sight.

The vile creature drew up in front of the store, dismounted with more curses, and tied his horse before staggering in.

"Where's the confounded dentist?"

He didn't really say "confounded."

Mr. Johnson stepped from behind the counter, dusting his hands.

"At your service." He nodded to the barber's chair in the corner. "Have a seat."

Mort Black stomped to the chair, or tried to. Every footstep made him wince. I had to stifle a laugh when he saw all those giant dental tools laid out. He might have run then, but pain won out.

"Mehitable!" Mr. Johnson hollered. "We've got us a customer. Looks like a nasty tooth, so we'll need something strong."

We'd agreed not to use Hildy's real name, just in case. Besides, "Hildy" sounded too cozy. We meant to scare the man, and make him helpless to boot. Maybe inflict a little pain in the interests of treating his ailment. We wanted to give him a taste of his own medicine.

Hildy's a sweetheart, but she's pretty big, a bit like me but more girl-like. There was no sign just then of girlish curves or sweet smiles. She wore a severe grey dress and a scarf over her hair, and carried a tray with her concoctions, several swabs, and a couple of terrifying implements of an unknown nature.

"Here you are, Doctor. The strongest we have."

"Sit, already!" Mr. Johnson commanded Black. "That looks serious. Sit down, I say, and open your mouth!"

Black still looked as though he wanted to run, but he sat, and Hank and Yance moved to stand behind the chair. They'd roughed up their hair and dirtied their faces and looked older than their seventeen years. They didn't need to look any bigger. Those boys make me seem right puny, these days.

When Mort Black saw them, he'd know he was in trouble.

Enoch Johnson looked into Black's mouth, and he stopped pretending. The smell, he told me after, like to knock him down. Pus oozed from around the abscessed tooth.

"Mehitable!" he barked. "My strongest disinfectant!"

Hildy offered a vial that I knew would cleanse a wound—but would sting like mad in the process, and tasted unspeakably vile. When Mr. Johnson swabbed some onto the infection, Black bit down hard on the swab—and nearly got the dentist's fingers.

Bellowing in pain, Black tried to lunge from the chair, but two pairs of strong hands gripped his arms.

"That tooth must come out now, or you're a dead man." There was no doubting that Enoch Johnson spoke the truth, and even Mort Black could see it. He moaned a little, but stopped struggling.

Mr. Johnson took up the horse tooth extractor, then shook his head and put it back, taking a more reasonably sized forceps. Black relaxed a little and let the dentist reach into his mouth again.

At that point, I got careless and Black spotted me, peering from the back room. Fury, and pain as Mr. Johnson grabbed that bad tooth, lent him the strength to tear loose of the boys and leap from the chair.

"It's a set-up! Yer no dentist! Yer jest tryin' to get at me. That, that creature put you up to it!" He was drooling in his rage, blood and spit and pus running out of his mouth.

For a moment, I thought he would come at me, and I stepped forward to give myself room to move, dropping into a defensive stance. If he tried to touch me, I'd kick that infected tooth down his throat.

Mr. Johnson stepped toward him. "Really, Mr. Black, you need. . .".

Mort Black turned with a snarl that might have been a sob, and ran for the door.

Tom waited there, at his post. He was supposed to keep Black from getting away, but he opened the door and stepped aside. If he had assisted Black with a kick on the backside, he could scarcely have sped him any faster than he already moved.

Black leapt on his unsuspecting horse and turned to ride back toward Endoline. A row of jeering youths blocked the way. A few girls were there, too, though they stayed behind the boys. All were laughing and shouting insults about Black's chicken-hearted response to a little old bad tooth.

He pulled up so hard his horse reared and spun around. Black appeared to be foaming at the mouth. I believe there was some soap in the disinfectant Hildy had given him. Enoch Johnson stood in the door of the Mercantile, still holding the forceps—and the rotten tooth.

"He should've let me clean it," he said.

The last we saw of Mort Black, he was riding like one demon-possessed, headed down the mountain away from the jeering youths. A curse on butchers who called themselves dentists floated back to us before he disappeared from sight.

The young of Endoline, and I think a fair number from Skunk Corners, let their laughter pursue Black, drowning out the curses.

I had a feeling we'd seen the last of Mort Black. No one on this mountain would let him forget he'd run from a dentist, and one thing I knew: a fellow like that could stand near anything but being laughed at.

21 THE NINJA LIBRARIAN AND THE NINJA LIBRARIAN

The delightful spring morning held no hints of the unnerving events that would unfold before night.

Our town purred along like a well-tuned locomotive that May. For once I wasn't even worrying about Billy Jenkins, since with the melting of the snow, his trips to the mountains with his pa had become both uneventful and a delight to the boy.

I should've guessed something was wrong when we had our Friday spelling bee, and Peggy Rossiter didn't win. But Janey Holstead did, and she's getting to be almost as good with words as Peg is with numbers, so I thought nothing of it. And Peggy, as usual, stumped me with her algebra lesson. I had no wish to fret, and I didn't.

It wasn't until school let out that the first sign of

trouble forced its way to my attention. And I wasn't rightly sure I should call it trouble, but it surely troubled my mind and my heart.

Peg stuck around after the other students left, and when I took a good look at her, I knew my unease wasn't just because Janey had won the spelling bee. Peggy Rossiter had something on her mind. And, like it or not, I was about to find out what.

"Teacher, we got Mrs. Herberts elected mayor."

"Uh huh." I didn't know where this was going and wasn't committing myself until I did.

"Even though she's not a man."

"Uh huh."

"So why aren't things more different?"

"What do you mean?"

"Well, it doesn't seem like much of anything has changed here."

"We got new books and they fixed the windows. What do you want?" I should have known the girl had something particular in mind when she'd picked our new mayor. Something more than just an election.

"Well, we maybe could have more books and keep the street a little more clear of horse apples."

Give me patience. She could lie better than that! "That's not what's worrying you." I had a feeling I could see it, just a glimpse of what troubled the girl.

"More books really would be nice," she said, her face so earnest I nearly laughed.

"Out with it. What's eating you so much you misspelled 'reprehensible'?"

She couldn't help grinning. "I guess I wasn't giving it my full attention."

I waited. Peg was thirteen now, not so much younger than Franny, and soon to be a young woman, despite her tomboy ways. I wanted to know what made that unusual mind work.

"No one treats women the least bit different than before. Mr. Burton still thinks it's a waste to educate girls, and he still thinks we can't learn math, even though I'm pretty sure I'm proving him wrong. He'd take MaryBeth out of school if you hadn't told everyone about the law and having to stay in school until you're fourteen. Half the folks here expect their girls to marry at fifteen, and the other half want them to just shut up and sit at home and sew patchwork!"

She was leaking tears of anger and distress, though she didn't seem to know it.

"When do you turn fourteen, Peg?"

Now she looked just plain miserable. "Next fall. And Pa says that's it for school. He says I needn't even start in September, and it's time I learned something useful, like cooking and sewing." She made a face. Then, seeing my look, she added, "Oh, he's not stupid. He knows I'm good with math and all. He just says he can't see any future in it."

"And you hoped that electing Mrs. Herberts would show him that women can do and be anything men can."

"Yeah. But it hasn't done any good. They still won't hire women anywhere but Tess's. And that's not what I want. Oh, Miss Tess is grand, but I want to learn more. I want to spend my time with *numbers*."

"You want to be a mathematician." My heart sank. Even if Peg could get her way with her Pa, she'd have to go away to learn what she wanted to know. But would anyone out there let her study math all day, any more than her father would?

What would Skunk Corners be like if she did leave?

Though I normally take all my perplexities to

the Ninja Librarian, this was one problem I didn't want to bring to him. I'd like to say that was because I wanted to solve it myself. But the truth is, I knew what was needed—and I didn't want to do it. Ninja Tom might actually know how to make it happen.

Instead, I went to Mrs. Herberts—we'd made an effort to call her "Mayor Herberts" at first, but we gave up soon enough because she just didn't need it. Anyway, I went to her with Peg's other questions, about what she was doing for the town. I was going to ask Tom first, but he'd gone up to Endoline. He and Ryan were making a branch library up there in the old barn they used as a schoolhouse.

Since Mort Black had been chased from the mountain by his own fat head and the laughter of a bunch of children, folks in Endoline had been coming around to the idea that maybe some learning wouldn't be all bad, especially for the boys.

It was a start.

"But why is everyone so sure girls can't learn, or work, or do anything but cook and clean and mind children?" I asked.

"Well," Mrs. Herberts began, but I wasn't done.

"We elected you mayor, so I thought people finally understood. But here's Peggy, better at math than anybody I ever saw, and her Pa wants her to stop school and learn to cook!"

Mrs. Herberts laughed. "My dear, learning to cook is always a good idea, male or female."

I knew that. My own cooking had improved, though I still preferred Annie's. But no one said boys had to give up everything else to learn cooking. Look at Tom.

Before I could rant further, Mrs. Herberts

continued, "But you are right, Alice. It's not the be-all and end-all of learning, boy or girl. As for this town, I think they only elected me because they were fed up with Mr. Burton putting on airs. And folks didn't figure mayor of Skunk Corners was a real job."

"Is that why you haven't changed things?" As soon as I said it, I worried that it might sound like an accusation.

She didn't seem disturbed. "Oh, perhaps a little. But, you know, when I took a good look at our town, I found I didn't want to change much, after all."

I must've looked unconvinced.

"Really, Alice, is Skunk Corners so bad? And I did appoint a School Board, so you could have a better schoolroom and maybe a bit more salary," she said.

That last part hadn't really worked out, but I appreciated the effort, and the repairs to the school made us all happy.

"But a town the size of Skunk Corners doesn't need a mayor. We just have to learn to work together and do what needs doing."

Which, I supposed, was what we'd spent the winter doing. So maybe she was right, though she'd talked different last fall, wanting us to organize and change things. And didn't I always want to keep things the same? But I wanted people to stop telling girls they were stupid and to let me alone if I preferred boys' clothes and living on my own over taking on some man and wearing skirts.

I left Mrs. Herberts, little satisfied, and made for my usual refuge. Even if our Ninja Librarian wasn't in, I could take comfort from the books. And he would expect me to do my exercises, with him or without.

I let myself in by the back door and headed up

front to get a book. I came through the door and stopped dead. Suddenly, Peg's discontents were the least of my worries.

A strange man sat at the librarian's desk, rifling through borrower cards with a discontented expression.

Naturally, I took him for a thief.

Naturally, he took me for the same.

"What are you doing here?" His tone was icy and mine hot, but we both put force behind the question. After a moment he stood up.

He was bigger than me, and his dark hair was slicked back in what I supposed was the latest fashion somewhere. His gaze was as icy as his tone, and he wore a frock coat with a bit of black silk in the pocket.

"I am the new librarian. This library is not, at this time, open, so you have no business here. I suggest you leave at once."

My heart froze at the words. To my shame, I turned and left. I should have thrown him out, but I couldn't think past my fear that he told the truth.

With difficulty I refrained from dashing off to Endoline to assure myself that Tom was safe and well. Or that he hadn't abandoned us again. What if he'd decided to stay up there? Maybe he thought they needed us more. I couldn't argue with that.

I hated that I had run away instead of knocking the interloper down and throwing him out the door. Of course, if he'd come from the same place Tom had—wherever that was—I probably couldn't have done it anyway. But I could have tried.

Instead, I went back to the schoolhouse and moped. I kept one eye on the library and an ear tuned to the arrival of the down-mountain train. Tom had gone up to Endoline on the noon train, and I expected he'd be back on the 6:00, which would arrive sometime between 5:45 and 7:00.

By 4:30, I couldn't stand it and went to see Tess. Naturally, she knew all about the arrival of a stranger claiming to be our new librarian. She seemed untroubled.

"I'm sure it's a small misunderstanding. I've no doubt he'll clear out when Tom arrives and he sees we're well cared for."

When I brought up Peggy and her discontents, Tess looked more sober.

"Yes, that's a child who should have a chance to get off this mountain. We shall have to see, when the time comes."

With that unsatisfactory response I had to be content, because she wouldn't say anything more. Uncomforted, I went back to my room and took up a book.

I couldn't concentrate on *How to Teach Higher Math*, nor on Shakespeare's *The Tempest*. I finally fell back on Mr. Stevenson's *Treasure Island*, which wasn't hurt by me being unable to concentrate on my reading, since I knew it by heart.

I'd at last fallen into the book and stopped looking up at every sound, when the door opened. I'd heard no train, and a glance out the window told me it was still too early, but there stood the Ninja Librarian. He carried his coat over his arm, so I guessed he'd walked down from Endoline.

I dropped my book. "There's trouble. Some stranger, claiming he's the librarian. He's got a frock coat and everything."

He nodded before I'd even finished. "Yes. I saw him as I was getting onto the train this noon. He," Tom added, "did not see me."

"And you just let him come and move right in?!" I didn't know if I was more astonished or angry. What right did he have to give in?

"I wished to think before I acted."

I wished I could say that's why I hadn't jumped the interloper. Maybe it was. I didn't pursue the point. "Fine. And now you've thought, what're you going to do?"

"I believe I'll have a chat with the gentleman. Would you care to come?"

That must have been Tom's idea of a joke. I'd liked to have seen anyone try to stop me.

We crossed the street together, and Tom paused on the steps of the library to put his coat on and straighten his tie. Only then did he open the door and walk in.

I stayed a pace or two back, and moved to one side to watch.

"Good afternoon, Heathcliff." Tom sounded completely relaxed.

"Thomas." The greeting wasn't quite as cold as the one I'd received, but close.

"I understand you were sent here under the misapprehension that Skunk Corners had need of a librarian."

"Misapprehension?" The stranger pretended not to know what he meant.

"As you see, I am alive and well and have no plans to leave Skunk Corners."

"You were removed from this post by the Council. A Ninja Librarian must follow the orders of the Council."

"So I was." Tom sounded cheerful. "I didn't like my orders, so as you well know, I resigned."

"A Ninja Librarian cannot resign."

"Oh?" A single syllable and a raised eyebrow told me more than it seemed to tell this Heathcliff fellow.

He continued to argue. "My instructions are to send you back and take your place."

I or any of my students would have responded

with a sneered "You and what army?" I waited to see what a Ninja Librarian would say.

Tom raised his eyebrow again. "You and what army?"

That must not have been what they usually say, because Heathcliff froze, confused for just long enough. Tom stepped across the room and picked him up from behind the desk.

What followed was something like what happens when two irritable wolverines meet— fierce, wild, and too fast to follow.

When the movement stopped, Tom held the interloper in an arm lock, and the dark stranger couldn't make up his mind if he was shocked, sullen, or outraged. He should have considered himself lucky. At his point, Tom would normally have tossed a miscreant out the door.

"Alice," he said instead, "would you mind escorting Mr. Heathcliff to the train?" He deftly transferred control of his prisoner to me, making sure my arm lock was as solid as his own. Picking up a valise from behind the desk, he looked around.

A row of faces of all sizes peered in at the open door.

"Ah, Peggy. You might carry the gentleman's valise for him, as his hands are otherwise occupied."

Peg picked up the valise and followed me out the door and up the street, as did all the onlookers.

"You needn't hold me," the stranger growled. "I know when I'm defeated." A sly look told me he thought he could worm around me and go back for another go at Tom. I pushed his arm a little higher behind his back, just to let him know I could. He gave a little squeak at the pain in his shoulder.

His chagrin at being bested by a much older Ninja was nothing compared to the humiliation of being frog-marched to the depot by a girl.

Good. He could go tell that mysterious Council of his, whoever they were, that Ninja Tom was in Skunk Corners to stay, and we weren't taking orders from anyone.

We reached the depot as the train drew in, and I escorted Heathcliff into the passenger car. I deposited him in a corner seat, wondering if I'd have to ride along to make sure he stayed put.

While I waffled, Crazy Jake and Wild Harry Colson stepped up and sat down, one beside the man, and one facing him, effectively boxing him in.

"Afternoon, Teacher," Jake said. "We had the day off to visit home, and have to ride on back down tonight. We're happy to make sure this gentleman catches his train back East."

Harry gave me a grin that reminded me of the days when these two were pure trouble. Before the Ninja Librarian.

Our Ninja Librarian.

Peggy dumped the valise at the man's feet—on his feet, I think—and we jumped down as the train whistled and began to move.

The other watchers vanished, since the fighting was over. Peg and I walked up the street together.

"You know, Teacher," she said after we passed the Mercantile, "I'm gonna have to leave Skunk Corners sooner or later."

I nodded, glum as a wore-out plow horse.

"But you know," she said again, "I don't think I'm in any hurry. I'm not leaving here until I've learned everything you and Mr. Tom and Tess and all can teach me. This place," she looked around, trying to find the right word. Then she smiled.

"This place is kind of interesting."

I nodded. She'd said a mouthful.

ABOUT THE AUTHOR

Rebecca M. Douglass grew up in Idaho, Arizona, and Washington states, and now lives near San Francisco with her husband and two teenaged sons. Her imagination resides where it pleases, in and out of this world. After more than a decade of working at the library, she is still learning the secrets of the Ninja Librarian. Her passions include backpacking, hiking, books, and running and biking. She works at the library, volunteers in the schools, and drinks too much coffee while writing.

Other books by Ms. Douglass include *The Ninja Librarian* and *A is for Alpine.*

Visit the author at www.ninjalibrarian.com

Made in the USA
San Bernardino, CA
02 January 2016